Caitlin's Choice

By Kat Attalla

Digital ISBNs
EPUB 9781772990492
Kindle 978-1-77299-823-8
WEB 9781772990515

Print ISBN 9781772990522
Amazon Print ISBN 978-1-77299-824-5

Books We Love

A quality publisher of genre fiction.

Airdrie Alberta

2nd Ed Copyright 2017
1st Edition Copyright 2010 by Kat Attalla
Cover art by Michelle Lee

Her eyes flew open. She sat up slowly and wrapped the sheet around her body in a display of modesty that was eight hours late in coming to her rescue. Andrew was leaning against the window, looking like he had a lot on his mind and none of it pleasant.

"Good morning," she muttered, unable to meet his penetrating stare. What had she done wrong?

"Would you like to have breakfast? I need to talk to you," Andrew said. His words sounded ominous.

"All right." She scrambled off the bed, tripping over the bottom of the sheet as she gathered her clothes.

Several minutes later, she returned from the bathroom dressed in her skirt and blouse from the night before, slightly wrinkled from the wear. As she sat on the edge of the bed to slip on her sandals, she felt as if she had stepped into The Twilight Zone. The man positively scowled. What had happened to the funny, caring, sexy man she had met last night? Was he upset with her or with himself?

"Are you ready?" he asked.

Caitlin glanced at the phone and back to him. "I have to check my machine first."

He nodded and folded his arms across his chest. His serious expression left her fearing that he was about to give her a kiss-off. With trembling fingers, she dialed her answering machine and turned her back on the brooding Mr. Sinclair.

Thank goodness there was a message from her sister. Caitlin jotted down the number on a paper napkin in her purse. A souvenir of last night, she thought. Her heart thumped painfully in her chest. Did she want to save it after all?

With an apologetic shrug, she lifted the receiver again. "Sorry. I have to return an important call."

Andrew raked a hand through his thick auburn hair and nodded again. He poured himself a glass of water and leaned against the dresser while she made her call.

"Hello?" a male voice grumbled into the phone.

Caitlin moaned. She hadn't stopped to think about the out-of-state area code. She might be calling the west coast at five in the morning.

"I'm sorry. This is Caitlin Adams. Is Maggie there?"

Andrew's muttered expletive made Caitlin jump. She spun around quickly. Before she could question the cause of his displeasure, her sister's bubbly voice came through the phone line, catching her attention.

"Caitlin! What happened to you last night? I've been trying to reach you forever."

"What happened to you? You never showed up." And I've obviously made a complete fool of myself in your absence, she silently added.

"I got married last night. Erik and I tied the knot."

Caitlin cupped her fingers around the phone and whispered into the receiver. "What do you mean, you got married? I thought the wedding was next month. I figured I'd get to meet the guy before you married him."

"We decided to elope. I am now Mrs. Erik Sinclair."

Caitlin lowered her head. Sinclair? Sinclair? Oh, no. The same surname as Andrew. Please God let this be one of those bizarre coincidences, she prayed, but deep inside she knew she wasn't that lucky.

"Caitlin?" Are you there?"

"Yes. I'm here."

"Anyway, Erik's big brother was giving him a really hard time about marrying me."

She felt her hackles rise in defence of her sister. "Why?"

"I'm not from the right kind of family, I guess." Maggie's voice was pitched with sadness. "Anyway, when he sent Erik to Las Vegas on business, we decided to get married here on our own. I only wish you could have been here."

Caitlin felt her blood run cold. Maggie's words brought her out of The Twilight Zone and back to earth with a resounding thud. Erik's older brother was the disconcerted stranger across the room.

"That's wonderful, Maggie. I wish I'd been there too. I'll call you tonight. I was just on my way out the door."

"When are you leaving?"

"Tomorrow night."

"Oh, Caitlin. I wanted to see you before you left. A year is such a long time. I just found you after nine years."

"I really have to run now. I'll talk to you later." Caitlin hated cutting her sister off, but if she didn't get out of that hotel room soon she would be sick. Worse, she might do something violent.

Her meeting with Andrew Sinclair had been no act of fate. He'd known exactly who he was looking for; the sister of the woman he didn't think was good enough for his brother. What had he hoped to prove by seducing her? Last she'd heard, being a fool where a man was concerned was not genetic. She snatched her purse off the bed and gathered all the dignity she could muster.

"It's been interesting, Mr. Sinclair. You might want to call your brother and congratulate him on his marriage, since it's too late to do anything about it now."

As she walked past him, he reached for her arm. "You don't understand."

She laughed bitterly. "I understand, all right. Your family blood is a bit bluer than ours. That makes us good enough to sleep with but not good enough to marry."

"That's not true."

"You're going to talk to me about truth? All those pretty words you spoke last night about fate and kismet were nothing more than lies, and I was stupid enough to fall for them." Tears pooled in her eyes and she paused to take a calming breath. She would not cry in front of him. "Let me leave you some money for the hotel, since the pleasure was obviously all mine."

Andrew jerked his head up indignantly. "Don't be absurd."

"This entire experience has been absurd. Let's not change the script for the finale." She wrenched her arm free of his grasp and reached into her purse. "Oh, and don't judge my sister by my foolish actions. She has more brains than I do. And, hopefully, better judgment in men."

She tossed a hundred-dollar bill on the bed and waltzed out the door with her head held high.

7

* * * *

Andrew made no attempt to stop her. For someone so angelic looking, she was one tough lady. He glanced at the crumpled money on the bed and winced. How many times had he done something similar in his arrogant youth?

Not only had he wrongly tried to interfere in his brother's impending marriage, he had hurt Erik's sister-in-law in the process, a double insult to a brother he professed to love. Yet he knew instinctively Caitlin had more class than to mention the incident.

"Caitlin," he muttered with a trace of regret. She was the most exciting woman to cross his path in years. He had finally met a woman he could share his life with and had just blown any chance of a relationship.

* * * *

Caitlin sat in the lounge at John F. Kennedy airport and checked her watch again. Another fifteen minutes. She hated the overseas restrictions that required her to check in two hours prior to takeoff. She was left with too much time to kick herself in the backside for last night's folly. To spend the night with a stranger went against all her principles. Worse, she would likely meet up with Andrew again, since they were now related.

Not in the next year though, she thought in relief. Her contract with a design firm tied her to Singapore for the next twelve months. She couldn't have run any further from the problem if she had planned it.

"Caitlin?" Maggie's excited voice called across the lounge.

Caitlin turned in amazement and gazed at the sister she hadn't seen in nine years. "What are you doing here?"

Maggie sprinted across the long hall and into her arms. "I flew back early. I had to see you before you left. Oh, you haven't changed a bit"

"You have," Caitlin said with a touch of sadness. Her sister had been a child when she had left. Now Maggie was all grown up and a married woman.

"I've missed you so much. I can't believe I'm going to lose you when I just found you again." Her eyes spilled over with tears.

Caitlin had long since come to terms with the fact that her parents had disowned her when she left home in disgrace. Only Maggie had believed in her innocence. When she'd come in search of Caitlin, Maggie had been forced to choose between her oldest sister and the family she had left behind.

"You're not losing me. I'll be back in a year. And you can call me anytime."

"I wanted you to meet Erik before you left," Maggie moaned sorrowfully.

Caitlin glanced down the corridor. "Is he here?"

"No. He had business in Las Vegas, remember? His brother Andrew drove me."

Caitlin gasped and dropped her purse on the floor. "What?"

"Erik arranged for Andrew to meet me at Newark airport and drive me over here. He's parking the car. I made him drop me off in front so I wouldn't miss you."

Panic gripped her. She couldn't face Andrew again. Not yet. "I have to go now, Maggie. They're calling my flight."

She collected her purse and flight bag and walked quickly toward the departure ramp, with Maggie at her side. At the gate, she stopped to hug her sister. She hated good-byes, especially when she hadn't even had a chance to say hello.

"Don't you have ten more minutes?" Maggie pleaded.

"I wish I did. I have to go. I love you." Caitlin shouldered her bags and gave her sister one more hug. She was almost home free.

"Caitlin. Please wait."

Andrew's voice stopped her in her tracks. She lowered her head and took a deep breath. Hadn't he been content

9

with the damage he'd already done? Gathering the few remaining shreds of her battered pride, she turned back for a brief second.

"I have to talk to you," Andrew said.

She refused to acknowledge his expression of sorrow. "Go to hell." Without a backward glance, she boarded her flight to Singapore.

Chapter One

One year later

"Yeah, yeah. I know it was a long flight. I wasn't too thrilled by it either," Caitlin said soothingly. "Why complain now? The worst is over."

She didn't receive an answer, but she wasn't expecting one. Tyler wasn't what she would call a stimulating conversationalist. At a mere three months old, he didn't need to be. He wriggled in her arms, fretting. His auburn curls stuck to his damp forehead. She brushed his hair away from his face and cradled him closer.

Often she would look at her son and her heart would break. Tyler was the image of his father. In an ironic twist of fate, this tiny bundle of innocent love would always remind her how painful adult love could be.

She walked around the small, two-bedroom apartment, rocking Tyler gently in her arms as she continued her inspection of their new home. Her face lit up with pleasure when she saw the nursery with the rocking chair in the corner. Her boss had arranged for the apartment to be ready for her return to the States. She hadn't known what to expect, but she was pleasantly surprised.

Tyler demanded to be fed, and since she was his only source of nourishment for the next few months, she sat down to feed him. Tyler's needs came first, but she had so much to do. She had boxes to unpack and food to buy. And her sister was on her way over. They had been pregnant at the same time, but Caitlin had never found an opportunity to tell Maggie. Some things couldn't be explained over the phone.

One hour later, Maggie arrived in the sleepy Connecticut town. With a diaper bag slung over one shoulder and a carrier in her hand, she ran up the front walk. Caitlin met her at the door, gave her a hug, and then relieved her of one small burden.

"I hope you drove slowly with that little darling in your company," Caitlin said, lifting the tiny baby girl into her arms.

"This is Allison Sinclair. Meet your Aunt Caitlin."

She gaped at her niece in wonderment. With her dark auburn hair and wide eyes, Allison could pass for Tyler's twin. "She's beautiful."

"I know," Maggie returned proudly. "Look at you. Singapore must have agreed with you."

"It was different. If I never set foot in an Oriental restaurant again, it will be too soon. I have some news that might come as a shock for you."

"What?"

"Come on. I'll show you."

Caitlin handed Allison back to her mother and led them to the nursery. She gently lifted Tyler from the crib and held him up. "His name is Tyler."

"Yours?" Maggie squeaked out in shock. "Why didn't you tell me?"

"I didn't want to worry you." More than that, Caitlin had been afraid her sister might say something to Andrew.

"Oh, Caitlin. You should have told me! Where's his father?"

"He's not important I'm not involved with him anymore." She never really had been, she remembered sadly. She had allowed herself to believe in the magical delusion of love at first sight. In the cold light of morning, the spell had been broken and the magic had disappeared.

Caitlin shook her head. Would there ever come a time when she would think about Andrew without feeling a wrenching ache in her chest? How often would she be able to avoid family functions without raising suspicions?

"Earth to Caitlin." Maggie broke into her thoughts.

"Sorry. Were you saying something?"

"Should we let them play together?"

"Sure." They took the children into the living room

and put them on a sheet on the floor.

The nearly identical cousins rolled around awkwardly in their diapers. After pouring a tall glass of iced tea for herself and her sister, Caitlin sat on the floor next to the children.

"What are your plans now? Are you still going to work?" Maggie asked.

"I can do a lot of work from home. When I have to go into the city, I can strap Tyler on my back and drag him into the office for a few hours."

"Do you need some money?"

"No, I'm in good shape financially. I got a nice bonus when I completed the contract in Singapore." Even if she hadn't, Caitlin would never accept a penny of Sinclair money.

"Look, they've both rolled over onto their stomachs." Maggie carried on as if the act were an Olympic feat. Suddenly, she gasped. "They have identical birthmarks. Look at the tiny crescent moon above their shoulder blades."

"What's so strange about that? We are sisters, after all."

Maggie shook her head. "That's a Sinclair trait. Erik has it and—" She gasped again. "Caitlin!"

"What?"

"He's Andrew's son, isn't he?"

Caitlin felt the blood drain from her face. Had Andrew told Maggie about their night together? Caitlin had never expected her sister to make the connection. What was she supposed to say? She pretended to be interested in something going on outside the window while she tried to get her pounding heartbeat under control.

Maggie tapped her foot impatiently on the floor and repeated the question.

Caitlin sighed. "Andrew who?"

"Don't play innocent. I know you know him. He told me you met the night Erik and I got married."

"Is that what he told you?" Andrew had certainly developed a flare for understatement since she had last seen him.

"For goodness sake, he had to say something. You told the man to go to hell right in front of me the night you left for Singapore. That's not a parting comment to a stranger."

"Tyler is my son. My responsibility. Andrew made no promises and he owes me nothing. I don't want to discuss this again."

The finality in Caitlin's words ended the conversation.

She quickly changed the subject to Maggie's new house. Caitlin was relieved that her sister was no longer living in the Sinclair mansion. Erik's mother and sister had been very inhospitable and Caitlin had listened to countless hours of her sister's tears at the rude treatment she'd received at the hands of the Sinclair family.

Except Andrew. Maggie had sung his praises regularly. Caitlin had feigned interest while an unborn Tyler kicked up a storm in her stomach.

"When are you coming to see my house?" Maggie asked.

"Give me a few days to get settled. I have shopping to do, and no help."

"Speaking of no help, I called Mom when Allison was born."

"And she spoke to you?"

"Yes. Father was out, and we spoke for almost an hour. She asked about you."

Asked about her, but didn't try to contact her. She felt a deep pain where her heart had been just seconds ago. After ten years, the silence still hurt. "Wouldn't Mom and Dad just flip if they knew I had a baby out of wedlock? Then again, they probably wouldn't be surprised. They always did think I was a no-good tramp."

"Don't talk like that. I knew it wasn't true."

"Well, you were the only one who believed in me. And Tyler would only convince them they were right"

"You made a mistake."

"No. Tyler isn't a mistake." Falling for Andrew had been the mistake. One she'd pay for the rest of her life. Tyler was the light in the darkness.

"I didn't mean it like that. He's an angel."

"Except when he's hungry."

"I know the feeling." The sisters laughed then, and the tension was broken.

They talked for an hour before Maggie said, "I have to head back now. Erik and I are going out tonight and I want to get Allison settled before we leave."

"And I have a ton of work to do here. I'll call you when I'm settled at the end of the week. Happy anniversary." Caitlin helped her sister to the car, keeping a watchful eye on the front door.

Maggie grabbed her in a bear hug. "I'm so glad you're back. I missed you."

"Me, too. Drive carefully."

As soon as the car pulled out of sight, she darted into the house and slumped against the door. She'd never given much thought to her son's birthmark, other than that it was one of the many wonderful things that made him unique. Now it seemed it might be the undoing of her secret.

* * * *

Andrew waited in the living room while Maggie and Erik finished dressing. His date had cancelled at the last minute, leaving him the third wheel at the anniversary dinner for his brother and sister-in- law. He'd thought about backing out himself, but he didn't want to offend his brother. He had not made the two-hour trip to see the house since Erik had moved to Long Island one month earlier.

The sound of approaching footsteps caught his attention. He spun around to see Maggie descending the staircase. His heart skipped a beat. For one brief second, he thought she was Caitlin. He hadn't been able to get her out of his mind since she'd left the country a year ago. The look of pure hatred she gave him in the airport still haunted his dreams.

"Erik will be down in a few minutes. Would you like me to show you the house?" she offered politely.

"Sure."

15

"We'll start with the study. It's Erik's pride and joy. After Allison, of course."

Maggie led him down a long hall to the large paneled study and gestured for him to enter. As he stepped inside, the door slammed behind him with a bang. He turned quickly to see Maggie glaring at him.

"You lied to me," she snarled.

"What are you talking about?"

"Caitlin. You said you and she had words. You had a damned sight more than words, Drew."

He furrowed his brow in confusion. Why was she bringing that up now? "I didn't lie to you. I told you that I was against your marriage in the beginning, and I already admitted I was wrong. I thought we'd straightened that out."

Maggie leaned against the door and put her hands on her hips. "Then how did you end up in bed with her, Drew? That's not a place where much talking gets done."

Andrew felt as if he'd just been kicked in the stomach. After Caitlin's parting shot at the airport, he'd been convinced she would not mention the incident. "Did she tell you that?"

"No."

"Then what are you basing your accusation on?"

"A three-month-old boy who's the spitting image of his daddy, if you'll excuse my crass, backwoods expression."

For several seconds, he stared at Maggie as if he couldn't understand her words. His hands, which had been resting casually in his pockets, clenched into fists. "What?"

Her eyes blazed with fury. She took two steps into the room and stopped directly in front of him. "Is there a problem with your hearing or just your comprehension?"

"Why didn't she tell me I was a father?"

Maggie threw her head back and laughed. "You're incredible. Donating sperm doesn't make you a father. If I'd been in her shoes, I wouldn't have told you, either."

He rubbed his forehead, trying to focus his thoughts. A son? He had a son, and apparently Caitlin had no intention of informing him. "When did she get back?"

"Today."

"What's my son's name?"

"Tyler. He was born just days before Allison. Isn't that a coincidence? Just like the crescent-shaped birthmark on his back and his auburn hair. The coincidences go on and on."

Maggie's sarcasm rubbed salt on his exposed nerves. Was he to blame if Caitlin hadn't told him? Of course he was, an inner voice mocked. "I want her address."

"You should call first."

"She might not speak to me."

"She definitely won't. As far as she's concerned, Tyler is her son, not yours. So be very sure you know what you're doing, Drew. If it's just idle curiosity, leave her alone. Playing daddy is a lifetime commitment, not an amusing pastime."

"That's a cheap shot."

"And deserved. I know my sister. She wouldn't have slept with you if she hadn't felt something special. And it was all just fun and games for you."

"That's not true." The memory of their night together—the most intense, passionate, and exciting night of his life—made him flush. The less than noble circumstances surrounding their first meeting and his subsequent omissions had cost him a woman he really cared about, and possibly his son, as well.

"She didn't even tell me she was pregnant because I went on and on about how wonderful you'd been to Erik and me. I feel like a fool. Like I let her down in some way." She paused to wipe away a tear. "You have no idea what she's been through in her life. Just this once, someone should have been there for her."

Andrew reached for Maggie's arm, but she backed away. "I'll take care of them."

"Money! Your answer to everything. She doesn't need your money and she won't accept it. Just decide whether you want a relationship with your son. That's about the only thing she's likely to accept. And even that will be grudging, you can be sure."

There was no doubt in his mind about that. During the course of the past year, he had thought a lot about Caitlin and what he would say to her when they inevitably met again. He'd felt confident that, with time, she would forgive, maybe even forget, their inauspicious beginning. He could give up on that idea now. Nine months of pregnancy and three months as a single parent probably hadn't endeared him to her.

* * * *

Caitlin loved the smell of fresh-cut grass. She'd been very specific in requesting an apartment with a courtyard. She got even more than she'd hoped for. The quiet neighbourhood had many young families, and she knew instantly that she would be happy in this small town.

She stretched out on the thick blanket of grass and pulled out a dandelion. Tyler rolled over on his stomach and looked for his mother. The humidity was rising, and already the beads of perspiration were forming on his nose and forehead. She ran her hand across his face and he gurgled in appreciation.

"See this, Ty? It's a dandelion. Some people think it's a weed, but I'm telling you it's a flower. A beautiful flower. Just because something's free doesn't mean it has no value."

He clutched the flower in his chubby fingers and tried to put it in his mouth.

"No, no. We don't eat the flowers. We appreciate their beauty."

"Isn't he a little young for botanical studies?" The deep male voice startled Caitlin. She flipped onto her back and propped herself up on her elbows. The morning sun blinded her. She couldn't see his face, but she didn't need to. The voice was all too clear in her memory.

She put her hand above her eyes to shade the blinding rays. Why did he have to look so damned sexy? In the past year, she had gleefully imagined him gaining fifty pounds

18

and losing half his hair. No such luck. Time had only improved his handsome features.

"What are you doing here?"

Andrew took a step forward and stood directly above her to block the sun. "I think you know."

She jumped to her feet and scooped Tyler up into her arms. Without a word, she turned and headed toward home. She hadn't reached the front door when Andrew caught up to her, following her into her apartment. Why did Maggie have to interfere? She didn't want him knowing about Tyler, yet here he was, walking into her house as if he had every right. She scrambled behind the sofa, trying to put a physical barrier between them.

"I don't want you here."

"May I see him, Caitlin?"

She held Tyler possessively against her body. "Why?"

"He's my son, isn't he?"

"Are you sure you don't want to make him take a blood test before you commit yourself? Think of the legal ramifications you're setting yourself up for here. Girls like me are just waiting around for a rich guy like you to put us on Easy Street."

His mouth twitched nervously. He didn't appear to care for her tone of voice. But then, she didn't really care about his feelings when her own were in such turmoil.

"Do you want child support before I can see him? Is that the point?"

"The only thing I want is to see your south end heading north."

For a few seconds Andrew stared blankly, and then his face flashed with comprehension. Caitlin covered her mouth and feigned sorrow.

"I'm sorry. Maggie told me how you Sinclairs hate our uncouth country expressions. It must have slipped my mind."

"You're not being fair."

Where did he get off talking to her about being fair? As if any of what he had done to her had been fair! Did he think he could waltz right into her life as if the past had never happened? "Translation: Andrew isn't getting his way."

"I didn't mean for any of this to happen," he said defensively.

"Oh, Andrew. Let me lay your guilt to rest for you." Her voice dripped with concern. "You didn't force me into anything, and I sure as hell don't want anything from you."

"Then why all this anger?"

Caitlin was stunned that he asked such a question. He had selective recall. He remembered being there to father the child but conveniently blocked out the rest. "Because you hurt me. I won't give you the chance to do it again."

"Regardless of your feelings for me, he's still my son. I would like to see him."

Was he dense? Couldn't he take a hint, or did he choose to ignore the fact that she didn't want him in Tyler's life either. "If I agree, will you leave?"

"Yes."

She came around the sofa and stood in front of him, holding the baby out for his inspection. He stroked his thumb along Tyler's arm. The baby gurgled and smiled, apparently unaware of Caitlin's inner turmoil. Tyler, who normally didn't react well to strangers, appeared quite content. He clasped his tiny hand around Andrew's finger. If she weren't so furious about his unannounced arrival, she might have been touched by the expression of awe on his face.

"May I hold him?"

She exhaled deeply. What would it take to get rid of him? She would let him have his look so he could go home and pat himself on the back for a job well done.

"Sit down first."

He lowered himself into the reclining chair next to the sofa. She placed the baby in his arms and stepped back. Now would be a good time for her son to spit up on Andrew's designer shirt. Run through the diaper. Drool. Anything to bring home the reality of a baby. Unfortunately, Tyler was against her today. He behaved like an angel.

"I know his name is Tyler. What's his full name?"

Caitlin tapped her finger against her temple. "Figure it out, Andrew. My last name is Adams. I'm not married, therefore his name must be . . . Can you guess it yet? Tyler Adams."

"There's no need for all this sarcasm. I meant does he have a middle name?"

"Why all the interest? Since you're not going to see him after today, what's the difference?"

* * * *

Andrew bit back a retort. Since he had showed up without calling first, he had to make allowances. She was in shock. But if she thought he would accept the role of an absentee father, she had another shock coming.

"What makes you think I'm not going to see him again?"

"Because I said you're not."

He dismissed her statement with a wave of his hand.

"We can discuss that later."

Caitlin shook her head.

"There will be no discussion, now or later. Leave us alone, Andrew. You've done enough damage."

"What is his middle name?" Andrew asked again.

She mumbled the name under her breath and he raised his head to see her face.

"What?"

She brushed an imaginary spot off her shorts and looked away. A red blush highlighted her cheeks. "Andrew. His middle name is Andrew. Are you happy now?"

He returned his gaze to Tyler, who had fallen peacefully asleep, and smiled. "Yes. I'm happy now."

"I'll take him."

"Show me where to put him."

His authoritative tone left no room for disagreement. She shrugged and led him to the nursery. With more tenderness than he'd ever known he could feel, he lay the baby down in the crib. When he made no move to leave,

21

Caitlin harrumphed and stormed out of the room.

As Andrew watched her retreat, he felt his body begin to stir. God, she was beautiful. Long, tan legs disappeared under the frayed edge of her cutoffs; her slim hips swayed with the anger of her footsteps. He recalled the sophisticated career woman he'd met last year and compared her to the barefoot beauty with a ponytail. Which was the real Caitlin Adams?

For a few minutes, he simply stood admiring the baby. His middle name is Andrew. Why did a woman who glared at him with such contempt still feel the need to give their child a part of his name?

When Andrew finally joined her in the living room, Caitlin was leaning against the front door, which she had opened wide for his exit. "So nice of you to drop by."

He paused in front of her. "I'll call you in a few days."

Angry sparks danced in her green eyes.

"Am I not speaking clearly, or do you have too much wax in your ears? Don't bother calling me. I will not return your calls."

"Good-bye, Caitlin. You'll be hearing from me."

She slammed the door behind him.

Andrew pushed his hands into his pockets and walked to his car. He could have handled himself better, but he hadn't expected to feel such an intense physical pull to her after all this time. Nor had he been prepared for the protective instincts his son had awakened in him. In a few days, when Caitlin accepted the idea that he planned to be a permanent part of Tyler's life, he felt certain they could sit down and come to equitable terms about their own relationship as well.

Chapter Two

Her sister had been after her for days to come visit and Caitlin was glad now that she had. Maggie's house in East Hampton was a dream. Caitlin enjoyed the ride every bit as much as she enjoyed the view of the ocean from the back-yard patio.

Gazing out at the waves, Caitlin felt herself slowly starting to relax after days of tension. Andrew had left countess messages on her answering machine, but she'd answered none of them. He had a small case of conscience. He'd get over it.

"Caitlin, how come you won't return Drew's calls?" Maggie asked her over coffee.

So much for relaxing. "Whose side are you on?"

"You're the last person I'd expected to ask me to choose."

Caitlin looked away.

"I don't like what he did, but it doesn't change the fact that he is Tyler's father," Maggie said in a softer tone. "There are enough fatherless children in this world. If he wants to see his son, he has the right."

Caitlin shook her head. "He has no rights."

"Yes, he does, no matter how much you want to believe otherwise."

"I know that this whole situation puts you in the middle. I'm sorry if it makes for friction between you and Erik."

"Erik agrees with you. He thinks Drew's getting just what he deserves."

Caitlin placed her cup back on the table and sighed. "You make it sound like I'm doing this out of spite. I'm not. There's nothing between us. There never was."

"I don't believe you. You felt something for him, or

you never would have slept with him."

Caitlin flushed. For over a year, she had coped by ignoring her hurt, by refusing to admit that she had felt anything beyond lust for Andrew. She had denied her feelings until they really had seemed to disappear. But seeing him again . . . she couldn't let Maggie know how it had affected her.

"How do you know?" she said. "You hadn't seen me in nine years before you came to New York."

Maggie's expression reflected her sorrow. "I didn't have to see you. I thought about you every day after you left. I heard everything they said about you, but I knew it was lies. I used to get into fights at school defending you. You made my life bearable because I knew if you could get out, so could I."

"That was a long time ago. People change," Caitlin said.

"The colour of their hair, the size of their clothes, perhaps. But not their basic nature. If you didn't care about Andrew, he couldn't have hurt you so much. Maybe he can't make that up to you, but don't punish Tyler, too. Let him know his daddy."

"The same man who didn't think you were good enough for his family? This is who Tyler should use as his role model?"

"He's changed."

"The colour of his hair? The size of his clothes? Or his basic nature?" Caitlin threw back lightly.

Maggie laughed. "Shot down with my own ammunition. Will you think about it? For Tyler's sake?"

"I'll think about it." And then I'll dismiss the idea as ridiculous.

Apparently Maggie still believed in fairy tales. Valiant Prince Andrew was going to sweep in on his white steed and save the young peasant girl from a life of shame. Well, Caitlin had stopped believing in fairy tales about the same time she learned there was no Santa Claus.

She took another sip of her hazelnut coffee and sat back, determined to enjoy the view. Maggie started to say

24

something, but stopped abruptly when the maid came out to the patio.

"Excuse me, but there's a gentleman here to see you."

"For me?" Maggie asked.

"No, ma'am. Miss Adams."

Caitlin's head shot up. She lifted her shoulders nervously. "Did he say what he wanted?"

The maid shrugged. "He said he was to speak to you personally."

Caitlin rose and walked into the house. The young man was leaning against the wall near the door. He straightened when he saw her and read from the paper in front of him.

"Are you Miss Caitlin Adams?" he asked.

"Yes."

"This is for you."

She took the envelope from him and stared blankly. "What is it?"

"Consider yourself served."

Caitlin stared blankly after the young man as he left the house. Served? Why was she being served? She removed the contents from the envelope and started to read as Maggie came alongside her.

"That son of a . . . I'm gonna kill him."

"What is it?" Maggie asked.

"Andrew Sinclair is suing me for custody of Tyler. I have to appear before a judge in family court."

"I don't believe it. Let me see." Maggie took the papers and read them over.

Caitlin felt the blood rising to her face. She pounded her fist against the door. Andrew was suing her? He couldn't be serious. "I don't believe he would stoop that low."

Maggie put her arm around Caitlin's shoulder and squeezed gently. "He'd never win, Caitlin. The most they'd allow is visitation rights, which he's entitled to anyway."

"Think, Maggie. He has money. He can afford the best lawyers. Private investigators. Just imagine what they'd dig up! My own father disowned me."

"But it was lies."

Caitlin slumped against the wall as a sour taste rose in her throat. Ghosts from the past were coming back to haunt her. "I can't prove it. If my own family didn't stand behind me then, what chance have I got now?"

"You were never charged with anything."

Perhaps she hadn't been arrested, but the town of Weldon had found her guilty ten years ago, and she was willing to bet they hadn't put a statute of limitations on the anger they felt for her. Helping to prove her an unfit mother would give them a small measure of satisfaction. "Well, I think a lot of people back home would disagree, and it sure won't look good to a judge. Particularly when Andrew's lawyers could twist the lies to suit their needs."

"I'll speak to Erik when he gets home. Maybe he can reason with Andrew before it gets to that point," Maggie said.

Andrew Sinclair, reasonable? In a better frame of mind Caitlin might have found that funny.

"I won't hold my breath on that one. I have to go. I have to take care of something right away."

Disappointment spread across Maggie's face. "What about dinner tonight?"

"I'm sorry. I'll have to take a rain check."

She collected her son and was out the door before Maggie could lodge another protest. She had nothing but murder on her mind. Or something worse.

* * * *

Caitlin leaned back against the elevator wall and cuddled Tyler closer. She had just gotten him to sleep; maybe because he was aware of his mother's tension, he had cried all the way into the city.

How could Andrew be so cruel? She didn't ask him for anything. Anyone else in her position would have taken him to the cleaners without a second thought.

Caitlin tried to calm her heartbeat, but her thoughts continued to race. What did he hope to gain? Was there some victory in taking her child from her? She would disappear before she let that happen.

She could go back to Singapore. She had received

many job offers while she lived there and was sure that some of them were still open. Could the authorities make her come back?

The elevator came to a stop at the twenty-fifth floor and the doors opened wide. She picked up the diaper bag and walked out into the reception area of Sinclair Electronics. The plush, uptown offices bustled with activity.

"May I help you?" the receptionist asked.

"I'd like to speak with Mr. Andrew Sinclair," Caitlin forced out with saccharine sweetness.

"Your name, please?"

"Caitlin Adams."

The woman looked over her appointment calendar and then back to her. "You don't seem to have an appointment"

"No, I don't."

"Mr. Sinclair doesn't see anyone without an appointment"

"He'll see me. Just call him."

"I'm sorry, but he has a rather tight schedule today. Perhaps if you leave a message. .

"No, thank you." Caitlin walked right past the receptionist and into the hallway.

"You can't go in there," the woman shouted after her.

"Call security," Caitlin tossed back and continued her search down the corridors.

She walked through the maze of offices, pausing just long enough to read the names on the doors. The longer she searched, the hotter her temper rose, until there was not one ounce of reason in her. Poor Tyler was getting bounced around in his carrier as she moved quickly down the halls but she couldn't waste any time.

She finally saw the office at the end of a hall: Andrew Sinclair. President. Before she reached the door, a security guard blocked her path. She made one attempt to pass him, but he stood tall and put his hand on his gun.

"Excuse me, miss. You'll have to leave."

She raised her head defiantly. "What are you going to do? Shoot me while I'm holding a baby?"

A crowd began to form, watching them with morbid curiosity.

"Well, go on. Shoot me."

Her raised voice woke Tyler with a start and he began to cry. She lifted him out of the strap-on carrier and held him against her shoulder, patting him gently. The disturbance in the hall got the desired result Andrew opened his office door to investigate the commotion.

"What's going on?" he demanded.

"It's all right, Mr. Sinclair. The young woman was just leaving," the security guard said.

"The hell she was," Caitlin snarled. "Andrew, tell your rent-a-cop that this is not the shootout at the OK Corral."

Andrew stepped around the guard and smiled. "Ah, Caitlin. I've been expecting you."

She turned her head and looked at the large gathering of people. She was too angry to care that she was making a scene. "Is this your idea of a welcoming party?"

She hadn't meant the comment to be amusing, but the office staff got a big kick out of it. To her immense aggravation, so did Andrew.

"Why don't we step into my office?" He looked down the corridor at the large group of spectators they had attracted. "Don't you all have work to do?"

Andrew spoke and people jumped. The crowd dispersed quickly. She stormed past him into the office and dropped the diaper bag on the nearest chair. She needed a pacifier to calm Tyler, but she was having difficulty searching through the bag while Tyler flailed his legs. She turned to Andrew and unceremoniously dumped the baby in his hands.

He held Tyler awkwardly under the arms, away from his body. Caitlin furiously pulled things from the bag. When it appeared that she wasn't going to find what she was looking for any time soon, Andrew gingerly cradled Tyler against his chest and gently stroked his back until the crying stopped.

She halted her search and looked up. "I'll take him."

"I've got him. Have a seat."

She grabbed a clean diaper and took a step toward Andrew.

"I said I've got him," he repeated.

"I'm not deaf. But the wool from your suit will irritate his skin." She slapped the diaper on his free shoulder and pointed for him to move the baby to the other side. He shifted Tyler and sat down in a chair.

Caitlin prowled the room nervously. Without Tyler in her arms to keep her focused, she began to feel caged by the office. The hairs on the back of her neck stood straight up.

"Have a seat, Caitlin. I think we have a few things to discuss."

She threw herself into the nearest chair. Her body trembled with rage, but she bit her tongue. Often her mouth spoke without consent from her brain. She could not afford to lose control. "What do you want?"

"You know what I want."

"You want to take him from me," she accused him.

He shook his head and spoke softly. "No."

"Then what was the purpose of the subpoena?"

"You wouldn't return my calls."

Caitlin dropped her jaw in disbelief. He sounded like a jealous adolescent who'd been ignored by the homecoming queen. "So you decided to sue me?"

"You didn't leave me a choice. I want to see my son. If you'll be reasonable, we can come to some kind of agreement without the court's intervention. I'm not trying to hurt you. I just want time with him, too."

Even as Caitlin searched for a response, she knew she had to accept whatever terms he set down. She couldn't afford to have him drag up things from her past—a past she had tried too hard to forget.

"All right. You can visit him sometimes."

"When?"

"It's not like you can take him anywhere. He's still nursing. He can't be away from me for more than a few hours."

"So I'll visit him at your apartment. How often?"

Seeing that Caitlin had refused to return even one of his messages, he figured she'd make sure she was out every time he planned to see Tyler.

"I don't know. We'll work out some sort of arrangement. Maybe on a Saturday, when I have to do shopping."

"So what you're saying is that I can see my son when you need a baby-sitter, and only if it's convenient for you."

She inhaled slowly, as if trying to contain her temper. "That's not what I said. But I work, too, Andrew. Not all of life revolves around your schedule."

"One day a week is not enough."

"Well, how much time do you want?"

A lifetime. "I have a proposition for you. I want you to come live in my house—only until he's old enough to be on his own for a day at a time."

He wasn't sure who was more surprised, Caitlin or himself. He hadn't planned much beyond getting her to sit down and talk to him. What better way to spend time with his son—and Caitlin, too— than to have them both right there under his roof? The more he thought about it, the better the idea sounded, at least to him.

Caitlin, on the other hand, seemed to be in shock. Her eyes widened to twice their size. "Are you serious? It could be eight or nine months before he's weaned."

"You won't be a prisoner. You can come and go as you please. I'll have a studio set up so you can continue to work from home, as you do now."

She arched her eyebrow defiantly. "And if I refuse?"

"We'll let a judge decide."

Andrew followed her gaze and noticed she was eyeing the paperweight on his desk. She might not be a violent person by nature, but he had to wonder if she was considering cracking him over the head.

He didn't like to make threats, but she was so stubborn he had no other way to get her attention, and he wanted her undivided attention. Though she glared at him with bitter contempt, she was the most desirable woman he'd known.

"If I say yes, I want it in writing that you'll be entitled

30

to no more than visitation rights when he's ready. I don't want you trying to get full custody later on."

"Caitlin, I'm not trying to take your baby away from you. But he's my son, too. I need time to build a bond with him while he's still an infant."

Tyler wasn't the only one he wanted to build a relationship with, but his son would definitely be the easier one to get through to.

Caitlin twisted her fingers nervously in her lap. He could almost see the wheels spinning in her brain. She was looking for a way out. "What's your mother going to think?"

"I don't care what she thinks. It's my house."

"I'm sure she'll have a lot to say, regardless."

"I know my mother can be pushy and domineering, but so can I. You don't seem to have a problem telling me where to go."

She rubbed her fingers against her temple. "Can I think about it?"

"Take all the time you need."

"All right. I'll let you know in eighteen years."

The minute she cracked a joke, he knew he'd won. He was wise enough to hide his elation and his relief. He hadn't expected her to give in without a battle. Yes, she was hurt and angry, but she must still have some feelings for him. Otherwise why would she have had the child when there were other options she could have exercised? Why had she named him Tyler Andrew? And why had she caved in to his offer so easily?

He lifted Tyler up into the air and jiggled him lightly. "What do you think, sport? Do you want to come live in your father's house for a while?"

Andrew got his answer in a line of drool on his suit.

Caitlin laughed and raised a victorious fist. "Yes. That's my boy. Shake him a few more times and maybe he'll spit up on you, too."

He wiped a handkerchief across his jacket and grinned. "You're spiteful."

"Me? You wrote the book, chapter and verse."

31

Spiteful? Was that how she saw him? He wasn't motivated by spite. On the contrary, he was struggling to do the right thing. In his entire life, he had never given of himself. In his arrogance, he had never looked back to see the people he had hurt in his climb to the top. His treatment of Caitlin had forced him to take a long hard look at himself, and he didn't like what he saw. He was thirty-six years old. Time to grow up. That meant taking care of his son and Caitlin, too, even if it was the last thing she wanted from him.

His gaze slid over her, taking in the long dark hair that tumbled over her shoulders, the delicate swell of her breasts beneath her blouse, and the long lines of her legs crossed at the ankle. Emerald eyes, sparkling with anger, met his stare without blinking. This was the image that had haunted him every night for the past year. A fiery, passionate spirit encased in cool beauty.

Maybe, just maybe, before the nine months was over, he could break through that granite wall she had erected to keep him at a distance.

Chapter Three

Caitlin sat next to Tyler in the backseat of the Mercedes and fumed. She was perfectly capable of finding her way to Andrew's house, but the Lord and Master had insisted on driving her and having her own car delivered later. Her stomach muscles contracted.

Why had she allowed him to scare her into this baby bargain? A judge wouldn't really give custody of a nursing infant to the father, no matter what the mother's past. Would he? She sighed. She couldn't afford to fight Andrew, and she wouldn't take the chance that she might lose.

She leaned back into the supple leather seat and gazed out the window. The murky waters of the Hudson River were a perfect foil for her melancholy mood. Nine months. Surely she could put up with anything as long as she knew the situation was temporary.

Several times she noticed Andrew watching her in the rearview mirror. His narrowed eyes reflected a strange sadness. Was he questioning the wisdom of his actions? Was there any chance she could get him to back down?

"Would you like to stop somewhere to eat?" he asked.

She glanced at Tyler. He was awake and fidgeting in the seat. Any minute his tiny lungs would open up at full volume to demand lunch.

"I have to feed Tyler. Can you stop at a rest area?"

"You need to make a bottle?"

"No, he breast feeds. I can't take him out of the seat while the car is moving."

She looked up and caught his reflection in the mirror. He was actually blushing! "What did you think I meant when I told you he was nursing?"

"I didn't think about it. I thought you were making excuses, so I didn't really listen."

Resentment burned through her like a fever. How typical of him to listen to no one and hear only what he wanted to hear. "We'd better get something straight. When I say something concerning my son, listen. If that's too difficult, then take me back to my apartment."

"Caitlin . . ."

"I'm not finished. Biologically, you are Tyler's father, so maybe that gives you some say in his life. But I will take care of my son any way I see fit. Is that clear?"

"You act as if I'm trying to crucify you. You know as well as I do that a year from now will be too late to form a bond with him. I know it's asking a lot for you to change your life to suit mine, but it's only for a short time. I don't mean to trivialize your job, but you can work from anywhere."

"I'm not talking about my work. I have to maintain some control over my own life."

He expelled an exasperated grunt. "I told you, you're free to come and go as you please."

"I'm talking about while I'm in your house."

"When it comes to Tyler, you call all the shots. Does that make you feel better?"

"Yes. Now find a place to pull over before Tyler starts screaming. He can be very distracting if you're trying to drive."

Andrew pulled the car off the highway into a rest area. On Caitlin's instructions, he chose the far end of the parking lot.

"Are you going to do it in the car?"

"Do it? I'm not having sex in the backseat, I'm nursing a baby."

She shook her head. The idea of breast-feeding in a public place didn't thrill her, either, but she had no choice. Already Tyler had begun to cry, and the piercing sound shot a pain to her breast.

Andrew got out of the car, looking embarrassed and uncomfortable.

34

Caitlin moved to the front seat, which had more room. She ran a sweeping gaze over the area, then opened her blouse and bra and shifted Tyler into position. Once he started to suckle, she closed her eyes and relaxed into the bucket seat.

She was almost asleep when she felt a feather light stroke on her breast. Her eyes flew open and she gasped. Andrew had reached through the window to run his hand along Tyler's cheek.

"What are you doing?" she muttered.

"Does it bother you if I watch?" he asked softly.

She lowered her head. "No . . . yes ... I don't know."

His desire to watch didn't unnerve her nearly as much as her lack of embarrassment. It felt right to share this kind of moment with him.

How could she indulge herself in these warm feelings toward Andrew? He had blackmailed her into living in his house, and he could change the terms when he wanted. Keeping her guard up was going to be difficult when the man could fluster her with just a touch.

"If that's a multiple choice, I take no." Andrew crouched down next to the car door and observed the simple ritual of life with curious fascination. For a fleeting moment, he felt a twinge of jealousy toward his son, but the feeling was quickly replaced by one of awe. Tyler was a part of him. Perhaps the only good part of him.

"How often do you feed him?"

"About every three hours, but he goes longer at night. If I'm lucky, he even sleeps through the night feeding. If not, I get up at around two or three a.m."

"I guess having Tyler around will force me to change my routine," he said.

"Having a baby is a lifestyle change, not just a change of routine."

"I realize that."

She shook her head as if she didn't believe him. "I'll give you credit. You had dead aim. Not everyone gets so lucky on their first try."

35

He accepted the personal attack silently. The things that came out of her mouth! Like a porcupine, she raised her quills when he got too close. Still, she didn't seem to have any regrets about Tyler or the lifestyle change it meant for her.

"Do you want to burp him?" she asked.

She must have expected him to refuse, because her eyes widened in surprise when he opened the car door to take the baby from her. Tyler was reluctant to let go so soon. He let out a small cry before Andrew cuddled him closer.

"I don't blame you, kid," he whispered to his son.

Caitlin flushed scarlet. Awkwardly, she fumbled to straighten her clothing.

"Just for the record, Caitlin, how do you know it was the first try? If memory serves me correctly, there was more than one shot."

She coughed and turned her head away. She could ignore the question, but she couldn't hide her reaction. Every inch of her exposed skin had reddened. So she did remember the night clearly, despite the champagne. He was beginning to wonder if she had any good memories of him.

What he'd done was wrong, but he could no more have stopped himself than he could have stopped breathing. She was so passionate and uninhibited that one year later he still remembered every second of their time together and every curve of her body that had filled out perfectly with the birth of their son.

She had every reason to hate him, yet here she was. The fact that she agreed to his demands meant she wasn't indifferent to him. Certainly she couldn't have been afraid of a custody suit. He had no grounds to take Tyler away. She was a gentle and loving mother.

Andrew returned Tyler to his car seat. When he came around to the front, he was pleasantly surprised that Caitlin didn't move into the back. Instead, she closed her eyes and sank into the seat.

"Are you all right?"

"Just tired."

"I guess getting up at two a.m. will do that to you."

"Packing and unpacking three times in two weeks will do it, too."

"Look at the bright side."

She raised her brow in a sceptical arch. "You mean there is one?"

"You'll be able to settle in for a long while."

"What a comforting thought."

He wasn't sure if she was serious or sarcastic, but he didn't ask. He had to handle her carefully. She still had the option to leave whenever she wanted. In the best of circumstances, he had a long, uphill battle winning back her trust. The living conditions he offered might be considerably more affluent than she could afford, but Caitlin wasn't a woman swayed by material possessions. So what did it take to reach her? He spent the silent, forty-five-minute ride to the house pondering the question.

* * * *

Caitlin surveyed the landscape in numbed shock. What had she gotten herself into? Although her sister had described the enormous contemporary house, Caitlin was still unprepared for the vast estate. The plush, green, manicured lawns were edged by magnificent flower beds. Their sweet fragrance hung in the air. A babbling brook ran along the west end, a wooden foot bridge spanning its width.

She was impressed, and she hadn't stepped inside yet. With Tyler in her lap, she sat on the grass and inhaled the scent of the peonies in full bloom. The kaleidoscope of vibrant colours caught Tyler's attention, and he reached out for a large blossom.

"Shall we go in?" Andrew asked.

"In a minute." She was stalling for time. Once she stepped inside, she was committed to go through with the deal. Her stomach muscles clenched painfully. She hadn't

37

felt this apprehensive since she'd found out she was pregnant and alone in a foreign country.

He crouched down next to her. "What are you afraid of?"

"Have you ever lived alone, Andrew?"

"Briefly, after college."

"Well, I've been on my own for the last ten years. I didn't have to worry if I offended anyone because there was no one to offend. Now I have to contend with your mother, your sister, and a full house staff."

He grinned. "You forgot about me."

She tried to ignore the warming sensation his smile caused. "I don't care if I offend you."

Andrew chuckled. "I asked for that."

She looked away, focusing her gaze on the pink and white flowers as she spoke softly. "Put yourself in my place. Do you think it's easy to walk in there under these circumstances?"

"I don't imagine it is. But the hardest part is walking through the door. It can only get easier after that."

With a shake of her head, Caitlin rose and walked with him to the house. "I never would have figured you for a closet optimist."

Andrew pushed open the massive oak doors. She cuddled Tyler against her body for comfort while fighting the compelling desire to turn and run. Her sandals clapped along the highly polished wood floors. Shimmering beams filtered through the skylights, casting geometric patterns on the central staircase.

She glanced down at her simple brown slacks and cream-coloured blouse, feeling underdressed. Andrew's house would never feel like home to her. She found little consolation in the fact that he didn't look at ease, either. Was he having second thoughts? Perhaps for all his brave talk, he, too, questioned the wisdom of this arrangement.

She followed him down a long hallway to the family room. It was so beautifully decorated, she felt she was in a museum rather than a home. Thankfully, she and Tyler would be gone before her son began to walk. She would never be able to baby- proof a house like this.

The far wall of floor-to-ceiling windows overlooked an Olympic-sized swimming pool. A small gathering of men and women lounged around the redwood deck, drinking and laughing loudly.

"We've arrived at a bad time," she said, waving her hand in the direction of the party.

"That's Leslie and a few of her friends. They hang around here often during the summer. I'm sure you'll get along famously."

Not in this lifetime. She knew from Maggie that Andrew's younger sister was a willful, spoiled princess who had never worked a day in her life. Leslie and her friends had taken a fiendish delight in mocking Maggie's accent and expressions until she had felt so out of place she had considered going to a voice coach.

"Caitlin?"

She shook her head. "I'm sorry. Did you say something?" Her arms had begun to tire, so she shifted Tyler to her hip.

Andrew came over and relieved her of the baby. His fingers brushed over her arm, sending a current of heat through her. Startled by her reaction, she took a step back.

"Would you like to see the house?" he asked.

"My room and Tyler's, please."

He shrugged apologetically. "Ah, I have to do a bit of rearranging first. I didn't realize you had to get up in the middle of the night to feed him. The nursery is on the opposite end of the floor from your room."

"Who has the room next to the nursery?"

"It was the nanny's room."

"That will do fine."

"It's very small."

She lifted her shoulders, unconcerned. "I'm only going to sleep there."

He frowned as though he would refuse, and then nodded. "I'll speak to the maid about having it prepared."

"When will my car be delivered?"

"It's already here."

39

Caitlin made a face. "That's impossible. We left it at the apartment."

"That was a rented car. I had the rental company pick it up and I leased another car for you to use while you're here."

"Without asking me?" she yelled, and then lowered her voice when she saw Tyler squirm in his father's arms. "This is precisely what I meant about keeping control over my own life. You had no right."

"I don't want my son riding around in one of those tin boxes. You needed something bigger, safer."

"What did you lease, a tank?"

"No. A Volvo."

"Are you out of your mind?" she snapped. "I can't afford the payments on that."

"You're not paying."

Caitlin bristled. That's just what he wanted, something else to hold over her. She should have known better than to leave the arrangements to him. "I can't take a car from you, even if it is only leased."

His jaw tightened, but he kept his voice level. "You are so damned stubborn. You have to disagree with everything I try to do."

"I'm here, aren't I?" she noted, tossing up her hands to emphasize her point.

"You made me threaten you. I had to serve you with a subpoena before you answered my calls."

"Are you going to have me arrested if I refuse the car?"

His face flushed in anger. He opened his mouth to answer her charge, but clamped it shut again when she began to laugh. "What is so funny?" he muttered through clenched teeth.

She leaned against the sectional sofa and crossed her arms. "You are. I can't win because you don't know what you want. You were willing to put an end to your brother's wedding plans because you were afraid Maggie might be after the Sinclair fortune, but you're ticked off at me because I won't be bought."

40

"One day that biting wit of yours will land you in trouble." He sighed and stroked a finger along Tyler's arm. "Do you want to see your room, sport?"

Andrew led them to the second-floor nursery. The brass crib and white lacquer furniture were the finest she had ever seen. The blue and white wallpaper looked brand new, and the shelves were filled with stuffed toys. Andrew certainly worked fast.

He walked over to the crib and Caitlin put a hand on his arm. "Don't put him down yet. I have to change him. Unless . . ." She held out a cloth diaper.

"Forget it."

She couldn't contain her smile. "I didn't think so."

He left, and Caitlin turned to the task of changing Tyler. As usual, he made it difficult, kicking wildly as she tried to put on another diaper. Once she finished, she placed him in the crib and rubbed her hand soothingly over his back to calm him.

"So that's him."

Caitlin whirled around.

A beautiful young woman stood poised in the doorway. Her haughty expression was underscored by her hands resting firmly on her hips. Dressed in a string bikini and five-inch heels, her red hair meticulously styled, she reminded Caitlin of some of the stuck-up models she had worked with over the years—a beautiful mannequin with nothing inside.

"You must be Leslie." Caitlin offered her hand, but her greeting was ignored.

Leslie stepped around her and walked to the crib. She gave one disinterested glance at the new arrival. "I guess he is Andrew's bastard. We had our doubts."

Caitlin squared her shoulders and remained expressionless. She would not give this self-centred witch the satisfaction of insulting her or Tyler. "I'm sorry you feel that way. By the way, his name is Tyler, not Andrew's bastard."

"You're not much like your sister, are you?"

"What do you mean?"

"Well, for one thing, she was smart enough to get Erik to marry her before she started popping out babies."

Caitlin cocked her eyebrow in amusement. "Does it come naturally, or do you have to work at being such a bitch?"

Leslie's jaw dropped open. "Who do you think you're talking to?"

"When you said I was nothing like my sister you were right. I can't be insulted by someone I care nothing about, so save your breath."

"You're pretty sure of your position here."

Caitlin shook her head. "I have no position here. This is a temporary arrangement at Andrew's insistence."

Leslie tossed her hair off her shoulder and raised her nose in the air. "Don't make yourself too comfortable. I give him one month before he gets tired of playing daddy and sends you packing."

"Only if I'm lucky," Caitlin muttered under her breath.

"What?"

"I said, oh, lookie. Tyler is ready for his nap."

With a grunt of frustration, Leslie stormed out of the room.

Caitlin leaned against the wall and exhaled slowly. She said a silent thanks to her sister for telling her what to expect. Andrew's mother and sister were a matching pair of vicious snobs.

Tyler began to cry fitfully, as if he could sense the tension. She stroked her fingers over his back in slow, rhythmic circles until he fell asleep.

"If we stick together, kid, we will survive this," she whispered.

But something Leslie had said bothered her. Would Andrew really get bored with playing daddy? She prayed it wasn't so.

For Tyler's sake, of course.

Only for Tyler's sake.

* * * *

Leslie dropped several ice cubes into a glass and filled it with straight gin. Tossing her head back, she took a large gulp. The bitter liquid burned a path down her throat. It didn't fill the emptiness she felt, but at least it numbed the pain. She glanced out the window to where her friends were still partying. Friends. While times were good, maybe.

She took another sip and reached for the bottle to replenish the drink as her mother came into the room.

"You're back from the club early. Couldn't wait to see the grandchild?" Leslie asked.

Joyce Sinclair smoothed her platinum hair and shot her daughter a stare that could freeze molten lava. "I am not amused."

No, Leslie could well imagine that her dour mother wouldn't be amused, but then few things in life amused her. Certainly not Erik's elopement with the younger Adams sister, nor Andrew's bombshell concerning the older one.

"I don't know what the hell has gotten into your brother, but he has gone too far." Joyce poured herself a glass of mineral water from the bar. "Have you seen him yet?"

"Andrew?"

"No. The child," she snapped.

Leslie finished off her drink. "Yes."

"And?" Joyce prodded, tapping her foot impatiently.

"He's a Sinclair."

"Never!" she growled out through clenched teeth. "I will never accept that . . . that . . . bastard into the family."

"I don't really see where you have a choice. At least until the novelty wears off for Drew."

Joyce twisted her fingers together until her knuckles cracked. "Then we'd better work toward making the novelty wear off sooner rather than later. Our livelihood might depend on it."

While Leslie didn't welcome the presence of Andrew's mistress and little bastard in the house, she didn't see that it affected her. As long as she wasn't expected to take care of the brat, it made no difference to her either way.

43

Considering her brother didn't think her capable of handling a file clerk's position in his company, she figured he wouldn't let her near the heir apparent.

She shrugged at her mother. "What are you talking about? You didn't have a problem with Erik's baby."

"Our financial security doesn't depend on Erik. It's bad enough Andrew has tied himself to child-support payments for the next eighteen years. But to plant the little gold digger in the house! Doesn't he realize this is a community property state?"

"Andrew's not stupid enough to get taken by a woman."

On the contrary, her brother was a master at manipulating people while keeping his emotions under control. His son was just one more acquisition to fawn over ... until the next new challenge came along.

"I hope you're not betting your future on the wisdom of the Sinclair men, Leslie. Your father was foolhardy enough to leave Garret in charge of the family finances. Need I remind you what happened?"

Leslie nodded, silently and sorrowfully conceding her mother the point. She glanced out the window at her friends still romping by the pool. She remembered another time and another set of companions. Companions who hadn't stood by her when most of the Sinclair fortune was lost. Perhaps her mother was right. Something would have to be done about Andrew's relationship with Caitlin Adams.

Chapter Four

Joyce perched on the edge of the wing-back chair, poised to strike. "Only one hour in the house and already she's making demands."

Andrew rubbed his throbbing temples. His mother's shrill voice had been rumoured to bring grown men to tears. She still believed herself the ruling matriarch of the family in spite of the fact that she now lived in his house. At times like this, he understood why Caitlin preferred to live alone. If Joyce weren't his mother, he wasn't sure he would even like her.

"It's perfectly reasonable to request a room next to the nursery so she doesn't wake the house every time she feeds the baby."

She groaned. "What possessed you to bring that woman here? If you had to do something, why not set her up in an apartment somewhere?"

He braced himself for another argument. His normally aloof mother had nearly had a stroke when she'd learned that he had a son and that he planned to bring Tyler to the house to live.

"This is my home, Mother, in case that slipped your mind."

"How will it look to our friends to have that kind of woman living here?"

Andrew drew his brows together. "What kind of woman is that?"

Joyce tapped a manicured fingernail against the coffee table, an annoying habit she indulged in while lecturing her children. "You know very well what I mean. The kind of woman who gets herself in trouble."

He exhaled deeply, trying to keep his temper in check. An attack on his own character he could handle, but he would not allow his mother to insult a woman she had never met.

"She didn't do it alone, so what kind of a man does that make me?"

"A damned stupid one." Disgust echoed in her voice. "Why weren't you careful? You're not some eighteen-year-old kid who can't control his libido."

Andrew let out a loud laugh. No, he wasn't some eighteen-year-old kid. He was a thirty-six-year-old man who had played juvenile games with a trusting woman. "She's here at my request, Mother. Actually, at my demand. You can make her feel welcome, or you can spend the next few months at the condo in Florida. I don't want any scenes like there were when Maggie was here."

Joyce raised her head indignantly. "I don't know what you mean."

"You know exactly what I mean. Did you think that Erik and I were blind?"

"You don't know anything about this woman, Andrew. Why did she show up now? Why didn't she make her unfortunate condition known while there was still time to do something about it?"

His fingers clenched into tight fists. Usually he walked away from this kind of conversation with his mother. Not this time. If he didn't stop her, she would be all over Caitlin.

"Tyler is not an unfortunate condition. He is my son. And whether you like it or not, they are welcome to stay as long as they like."

Her eyes narrowed as she glared at him. "What if she doesn't leave? Have you considered that? What if she decides she's entitled to half your estate?"

If only it could be that easy. Caitlin wanted nothing from him, which gave him no leverage in dealing with her. If she chose to leave, he couldn't do a damned thing to stop her. How long could he reasonably expect her to put up with a situation that he himself found strained, at best?

"If she asked for it, I'd give it to her. She's the mother of my son, who is my sole heir as of yesterday." He grinned. "So I'd suck up to them good if I were you, just in case something happens to me."

Joyce let out a horrified gasp, but she quickly regained her composure. "Don't be crass."

"Why not? That seems to be the only thing you understand. Don't make me choose between you. You might not like who comes out on top."

"Sounds like you plan to marry that woman."

The corners of his mouth curled in a smirk. "Would you like a good laugh? She wouldn't have me. She's only here because I threatened to sue her for custody if she didn't let me see my son." He spun around and walked out of the room, calling over his shoulder, "I'll see you at dinner—and I expect you and Leslie to be polite and welcoming."

Andrew left his mother stewing in the living room. His blood pressure had risen, as evidenced by the splitting headache that refused to subside. After speaking to the maid about preparing the small room for Caitlin, he went to the bathroom for his medication.

This was not what the doctor had meant by keeping his stress level down. He had finally begun to delegate the running of Sinclair Electronics to his executive staff so he could have calm in his life. He didn't need this aggravation from his family.

He swallowed the tablets with a large gulp of water.

Caitlin burst through the door, and then froze when she saw him. "Sorry, I thought it was empty ... I mean, is this your bathroom?"

"I'm finished here," he said and placed the bottle back in the medicine cabinet.

"What's that?"

"Vasotec. For hypertension. Nothing serious."

She leveled a questioning gaze. "High blood pressure is very serious if you don't take care of yourself."

He smiled at the hint of concern in her voice. "If you're so worried about me, then just agree to everything I say in the future and I'll have no problem."

"Better men than you have tried to play on my guilt

47

and failed," she shot back. "I'd better check Ty."

"I'll check him. You needed the bathroom. When you're finished, I'll show you around."

She backed herself into the wall to allow him to exit. Although he had plenty of room, he deliberately brushed his hip against hers to see her reaction. Caitlin's face remained an expressionless mask. The jolt to his system, however, was immediate and electric. He'd made a point, but not the one he'd hoped.

* * * *

Caitlin splashed cold water over her face and arms, then blotted her damp skin with a plush towel. She had drawn on every ounce of her strength to fight off a reaction until Andrew had retreated down the hall. Had her traitorous body forgotten the pain and humiliation of the past year, not to mention the blackmail of the past week?

No man had ever affected her the way Andrew could. She would fight to her last breath before she would cede that power to him again. He had damned near destroyed her the last time.

With her pulse rate back under control, she went to the nursery.

Andrew stood by the crib, arranging the blanket around Tyler. She hovered in the door-way and watched him gently stroke his finger along the baby's face. Perhaps Andrew was serious about having a relationship with his son. He gazed at Tyler with that same wide-eyed wonder she had often felt herself.

"Andrew?"

His brow creased. "You're ready?"

"If you'd rather stay, I'll explore on my own."

"No. I'll see him when he wakes up." He hooked his arm though hers. If he noticed her rigid tension, he didn't comment. "Should we start with your studio?"

Just off the library was a large room with a drafting table and personal computer. The stark white walls and clean angular lines of the cathedral ceiling gave the feeling of vast space. Caitlin knelt on the love seat below a bay window and basked in the warmth of the view. The wooden bridge she had seen earlier led to a charming Japanese rock garden. With this magnificent landscape to gaze at, she would never get any work done.

"Whose studio was this?"

"Mine. I didn't start life as president of Sinclair Electronics. I was an electronics engineer."

She turned and settled herself into the buttery soft leather cushions. "Oh. I thought you inherited the company."

"Only the money to start it. I built the business up from scratch. When Erik finished college, he joined me. It's been twelve years of hard work."

All right, so she was forced to revise her opinion of the pampered playboy. He had earned his money.

"What about you?" He lowered himself into the swivel chair and rolled it in front of where she sat. The spicy scent of his aftershave wafted around her, wreaking havoc on her senses. She couldn't think of a way to make him move without admitting that his nearness unsettled her. "What exactly does a fabric buyer do?"

Damn! He must have been grilling Maggie for information about her. Why? She bit her tongue to keep from asking in case he figured out she had something she wanted to hide. Perhaps if she volunteered some information, he wouldn't feel the need to dig further.

"I'm responsible for the design and quality of our fabrics. That's why I spent a year in Singapore, to set up the new factory. Most of our silks will be produced there."

"How did you get into something like that?"

She shrugged and made herself comfortable in the love seat for the abridged—and censored— story of her life. "I won a local design contest sponsored by a New York fashion institute. Five hundred dollars and a two-week intensive training program. My father told me I couldn't accept because my fiancé wouldn't approve."

"You were engaged?" he muttered in surprise.

"Yeah, it was news to me, too. My dad assumed that

since the banker's son took an interest in me, naturally I'd be dying to marry the only rich boy in the county."

"The banker's son?"

"I know, I know," she said with a laugh. "Right out of a Norman Rockwell painting. Anyway, I went against my father's wishes and came to New York anyway. I was going to be the next Coco Chanel. I thought New York was just waiting for me. Boy, did I get an education real fast."

His lips curled upward in a smile. "I'll bet."

"The two-week intensive training program turned out to be nothing more than an orientation. I didn't learn diddly squat."

He looked at her as if she'd grown a third eye. "What?"

"Sorry. It means I didn't learn anything."

"You don't have to apologize."

"Anyway, they wanted five thousand dollars a year for tuition. Suddenly my five-hundred-dollar fortune seemed like pocket change."

"What did you do?"

"What every country girl does when she finds herself disillusioned with the big city. I called home, where I was told in no uncertain terms that I was not welcome."

"Just because you refused to get married?"

"It's a bit more complicated. I'd rather not talk about it." A hollow ache constricted in her chest. Some memories still had the power to crush after ten years. She sucked in a deep breath and exhaled slowly.

"All right. What did you do next?"

Hoping to quell the rising sorrow, she tried to change the subject. "Listen to me. I'm running on and on. You can't really be interested."

"I am interested."

Too interested. If she refused to continue, she might pique his curiosity even further. "Well, I attended the orientation. That was where I met Marc Stevens. He was looking for models. So I thought, 'Okay, I won't be the next Coco Chanel, just the next Cindy Crawford.' Wrong!"

"Let me guess? He wanted to take art photos."

50

Andrew's voice was judgmental. Wouldn't he just love to have something like that to hold over her? "No. He wanted a human mannequin. I'd stand around while a designer tucked and pinned and cut. It wasn't Vogue, but it was decent and it paid the bills. While I worked at the design house, I developed a fascination for the fabrics, so I studied at night. The rest, as they say, is history."

"You never went back home? Even to visit?"

Oh sure. And get myself strung up from the highest tree. The town of Weldon, West Virginia, was just waiting for the return of its most notorious expatriate. The townsfolk had gotten swindled by their own greed, and they were out for blood. In leaving home when she had, she'd given them a perfect scapegoat. Innocence or guilt didn't matter. She had been judged by the company she kept.

She had never been indicted for any crime, but she also knew that Andrew would be able to find any number of people back in her little hometown willing to perjure themselves for revenge if he decided to sue her for custody. Tyler was the most important person in her life, and she would do whatever she had to keep him. If that meant living by Andrew's rules for a while, then so be it.

"Caitlin?"

She raised her head and met his curious gaze. "No. I've never been back."

"I'm sorry."

"I'm not. Tyler and Maggie are the only family I need."

Sorrow tugged at her heart. She could lie to Andrew, but not to herself. She missed her family, and she would have traded a year off her life for one day with them. Ten years had passed, and the loneliness still remained.

"Are you all right?"

She didn't realize she was crying. "I'm fine."

He brushed his thumb over her tear-stained cheek. "If you feel like talking . . ."

Caitlin waved her hand to cut him off. She had already revealed more than she'd intended, more than was wise. Inhaling deeply, she buried the painful memories the only

51

way she knew how, by erecting a wall.

"Life's tough. You fight or you give up. I'm not a quitter. I beat the odds. Do you know what happens to many young women who arrive in the city with no education or career training?"

"Unfortunately, I do. Maggie was lucky to have you."

"Not me, your brother. She was in a coffee shop, calling all the listings for C. Adams in the phone book, when she met Erik. He helped her find a job and a place to live, and eventually helped her find me."

"I guess the phone book didn't work."

"I wasn't living in Manhattan. When she finally did locate me, it was two days before I left for Singapore."

"That wasn't much time for a reunion."

"And you managed to cut that shorter by sending your brother to Las Vegas."

His nostrils flared at the mention of their less- than-perfect beginning. He didn't want to be reminded; however, she couldn't afford to forget.

"Shall we go to dinner?" he asked.

"What are my other choices?"

"It won't be that bad. I've already spoken to my mother, and she's waiting to meet you."

Hmm. Judging by Leslie's attitude, Caitlin was as welcome as a mosquito at a nudist camp. She rose and joined Andrew for the long walk down the corridor.

The huge, formal dining room was dwarfed by the massive furnishings. The teakwood table could seat twenty with plenty of elbow room to spare. A brass and crystal chandelier shimmered above a fresh floral centrepiece. The table was laid out in gold-leafed china. Caitlin was more intimidated than she expected. If this was a nighty routine, she would lose all desire to eat.

Joyce and Leslie were already seated when she and Andrew entered. Neither woman rose to greet her. Instead, Joyce tapped her Rolex.

"It's after seven, Andrew."

"And I'm over twenty-one, Mother. I am permitted to be late for dinner in my own home."

Caitlin bit her bottom lip to keep from smiling. Apparently Andrew didn't take criticism from anyone.

"This is my mother, Joyce. Caitlin Adams," he said.

"Hello, Mrs. Sinclair."

Joyce ran a sweeping gaze over Caitlin. "Miss Adams. How nice to meet you."

The words had about as much sincerity as a used-car salesman's pitch.

"And my sister, Leslie," Andrew continued.

"We've already met," Caitlin said. "She stopped by the nursery earlier to meet Tyler."

"She did?" he asked.

Leslie had paled slightly. He gazed toward Caitlin, as if trying to assess how much damage his sister had done, but her expression gave nothing away.

"Yes. She remarked on how much Tyler looked like you," Caitlin said. Or words to that effect.

Andrew grinned. "She said how handsome he was?"

"Please. Tyler is much better looking than you."

She had hoped the small joke would be an icebreaker, but Andrew was the only one who laughed.

"Ouch. No chance my ego will run out of control while you're here."

He pulled out a chair for her. She nodded and slipped into the seat.

"Would you like a drink?"

"Water, please."

"No wine? Or do you still prefer champagne?"

Caitlin lowered her head as a warm flush crept up her cheeks. His seemingly innocent question revived memories of their night together that she wanted to keep buried.

"I can't drink while I'm nursing."

Leslie let out a disgusted grunt. "How gauche. Do we have to discuss that at the dinner table?"

"What would you like to discuss?" Andrew asked, as he sat at the head of the table. "Something you know about, like shopping?"

Caitlin stifled a groan. It was going to be a long nine months.

Dinner proceeded awkwardly. The lobster bisque, which was prepared to perfection, held no appeal for Caitlin's churning stomach. She couldn't touch the salmon that followed.

"Would you pass the salt, Caitlin?" Andrew said to break the silence.

She handed him the pepper grinder. He wouldn't have corrected her, except Leslie snickered.

"That's the pepper."

"I know," Caitlin said simply. "Salt will kill you."

"A health-food fanatic," Leslie moaned.

A piercing cry erupted from the intercom in Caitlin's pocket. As she turned down the volume, he noticed the look of relief on her face. She placed her napkin on the table and rose.

"If you'll excuse me."

"Can we expect this interruption every evening?" Joyce asked.

"There is no interruption. I'm finished anyway." Caitlin forced herself to walk calmly until she was out the door, then ran down the corridor as fast as she could.

Andrew listened until the footsteps got fainter. Bitter anger rose like bile, leaving a foul taste in his mouth. He shot a furious scowl at his mother and sister. "Thank you. I know I ask so much of you in return for paying all the bills here."

"There's no need to raise your voice. Do you want the servants to hear you?" Joyce asked. "You've already given them enough to gossip about."

"I don't give a damn who hears me. Take a look at your own behaviour this evening. I guess it was too much to expect that you be courteous to a guest. The word doesn't exist in your vocabulary." He threw his napkin on the table and shoved his chair back. Completely disgusted, he stormed away. His mother's call halted him at the door.

"What?" he snapped.

"You haven't forgotten about the Forsyth's' bridge party tonight, have you?"

"I can't make it."

"You realize it is unspeakably rude to cancel at the last minute."

"You're going to preach to me about rude behaviour?"

He strode back to the table and glared at his mother and sister. Neither showed even a spark of remorse. "If you think your behaviour will make me reconsider the living arrangements, you're right. But Caitlin and Tyler won't be leaving." He kept his voice low, but there was no mistaking the warning.

Chapter Five

Andrew slumped down in the leather chair in his study without bothering to turn on a lamp. The darkness suited his present frame of mind. His family, who supposedly loved him, cared more about the balance of power than they did about him. Caitlin, who had every reason to hate him, worried about whether he put salt on his food when he was under orders to avoid it. How had his family deteriorated into this gathering of strangers?

His mother had become a nasty, bitter woman. And Leslie! She lived her life from the bottom of a gin bottle. At twenty-one, she looked older than Caitlin's twenty-eight years. Not that he had won any awards in the decency department himself. Until last year, when his treatment of Caitlin had given him a wake-up call, he had been no better.

"Andrew?" The voice was barely a whisper, with a hint of concern. That eliminated anyone in his family.

"Come in, Caitlin."

She entered the darkened room slowly. A diaper bag hung from one shoulder, and she held a portable carrier. The light from the hall allowed a glimpse of her delicate features.

"I guess this is a bad time?"

"No. What did you need?"

"Where is the car you leased for me?" She shifted her weight between her feet, and he could tell that she was uncomfortable accepting anything that came from him.

"In the garage. The keys are in it. Why?"

"I need a few things from the store."

He clicked on the desk lamp. "I'll drive you."

She shook her head. "It's not necessary. But you can

watch Tyler."

His anger dissolved in a wave of shock. "What?"

She placed the carrier on the desk. Tyler was intently studying an assortment of brightly coloured plastic keys that dangled from the crossbar.

"You can't leave," Andrew muttered desperately, grabbing her arm.

"You did say I was free to come and go as I please, right?"

She picked through the bag on her shoulder, then handed Andrew a bottle of water. He released her arm and absently took the bottle. "Yes, but . . ."

She dropped a clean diaper and a box of baby wipes on the desk. "And you did say the point of my being here was so you could spend time with Tyler, right?"

"Well, yes, but . . . wait a second . . ."

With a casual shrug, she backed herself toward the door. "You have a water bottle. If he cries, give him the water. If he's bored, entertain him. If he wets the diaper, change him."

"You can't do this right now. It's been a bad day."

Caitlin gave a little chuckle. "Do you think it's been a picnic for me?"

"No. But what do I do with him?"

"Read him the newspaper. Take him for a swim. Hold him, talk to him. Whatever you want. I'm going out."

"Don't do this to your son."

"If you truly can't handle him, you have two live-in staff members in the house. Ask one for help."

And with that, Caitlin left him alone with Tyler. He knew what she was doing. She thought that if he saw how much work was involved, he might think Tyler wasn't worth the effort. Well, he hadn't built a multimillion-dollar corporation by backing away from a challenge.

"We'll show her, sport."

He turned his attention to his son, who was oblivious to his mother's desertion. Jiggling the keys kept Tyler entertained for all of five minutes before he began to twist and writhe in the seat. When he started to cry, Andrew tried giving him the water, but Tyler turned his head from side to side and cried louder. Finally he took the baby, carrier and all, into the kitchen.

"What's wrong with him, Sally?" he asked the housekeeper.

"I think he wants to be held, sir."

"Right." But somehow the simple act of removing his child from the seat was beyond him. He pulled and tugged, but Tyler seemed to be caught or entangled in something. As his cries grew ever louder and more grating, Andrew cursed Caitlin with every swear word he knew. Damn her. He would die before he would admit that he couldn't handle Tyler.

Sally pursed her lips together tightly. When he looked up, she turned her head away and coughed. The servants were laughing at him. Could things get any worse?

"Okay. What am I doing wrong?"

"Excuse me, sir, but it does help if you remove the seatbelt first. It's just under the little blanket there."

"I knew that."

"I'm sure you did, sir."

Luckily he didn't pay the staff to lie to him. They weren't very good at it.

Once he got Tyler out of the seat, Andrew had no trouble handling the baby. He took his son for a stroll around the grounds and even for a dip in the heated swimming pool. For the first time in years, he felt completely relaxed and at peace.

Caitlin thought he would get so wound up that he would relent and let her leave. He showed her.

Or did he?

He couldn't imagine that she would use Tyler to punish him, even for spite. That wasn't her style. She must have known all along that being with the baby would relax him and lower his blood pressure.

As the last of the sun dipped below the horizon, he got out of the pool and wrapped Tyler in a plush towel. The house they returned to was hushed and peaceful. His mother and sister had gone out and the staff had retired. He had hoped his mother might show enough interest to take a look at his son, but even her attitude didn't bother him right now. Nothing mattered but Tyler.

And Caitlin. Caitlin, who looked at him with such anger and hurt, then treated him with such caring.

"So tell me, Ty. How do I get through to your mama?"

He lay Tyler down on the sofa and stripped off the soggy diaper.

"You don't know either? Here, sit on this." Andrew lifted Tyler's legs and centred him on the fresh diaper. "I saw Three Men and a Baby, sport. I know how to change a diaper. But let's keep that between us. There's no reason your mother has to know about any of this. She'd have me doing this every day as penance."

"Have you doing what?"

Andrew jerked his head up. Caitlin was leaning against the wall observing him with a grin.

"How long have you been there?" he asked.

"I just got back. I would have been back sooner, but I couldn't find one person who could direct me to the nearest Value Mart."

Andrew swallowed a laugh. The first person she asked probably wanted to have her arrested for breach of decorum. Ramapo Heights did have the most snobs per capita in the country. "That doesn't surprise me. Ask for directions to Tiffany's and you would have had more luck. What did you buy?"

"It may have escaped your notice, but Tyler doesn't have any clothes. They were packed in the back of the car you returned to the leasing company."

"Sorry. I'll pay you back."

"Forget it. I called and asked the company to send the boxes back."

She shrugged and held up the bag. "I just bought an outfit in case you have company, although I got the impression that your mother has no interest in showing off her grandson."

He lifted Tyler into his arms. "Does that bother you?"

"What bothers me is that Tyler won't have a

59

relationship with any of his grandparents. What a shame. He'll be missing so much ..."Her voice cracked. "I'll be back for him in a minute."

She turned and sprinted down the hall.

Obviously, she missed her family very much. Perhaps if he tried to bring them together, she would warm up to him. Of course, he had no idea how to find her family. Andrew's mind started racing. Here was something he knew how to do: set an objective, do research, and mount an attack. He certainly had nothing to lose by trying.

* * * *

When Caitlin returned to the living room, she found Andrew stretched out on the sofa with Tyler lying comfortably on his bare chest. Andrew rubbed his hand in circles over his son's back, winning a gurgling sigh of appreciation. She sat in the chair across from them and watched enviously. Did babies know instinctively who their parents were, she wondered. Tyler had taken to Andrew instantly.

But then, so had she, Caitlin reminded herself, and look where that got her.

"I think he likes me," Andrew whispered warily, as if the admission might break some invisible spell.

"If you were rubbing my back, I'd like you, too," she said without thinking.

Andrew laughed. "Is that a fact? I'll keep that in mind for when I'm done here."

"Don't be so literal."

"Caitlin, I know you're a bit angry with me right now . . ."

"A bit?" she repeated, mocking his flair for understatement. "That doesn't come close to what I'm feeling toward you."

"Then what was this evening about?" he challenged.

She shrugged. "I don't know what you mean."

He sat up, snuggling Tyler in his strong arms. "Yes, you do. You didn't leave Tyler with me to punish me. You knew I was hanging by a thread and you also knew that having to entertain Tyler would take my mind off my problems."

"You're crediting me with amazing insight."

"Why won't you admit you care? You agreed to come live with me when you knew very well I never could have won a case in court"

She twisted her fingers together in her lap. "That's not the point. I didn't have enough money to fight you."

"A first-year law student could have won that case. Unless you have a secret past as a felon, of course."

She didn't meet his grin with one of her own.

"So what about it Caitlin? You didn't really think that even the most liberal judge would have taken an infant away from his mother?"

"What's the difference? Tyler is entitled to have his father, if that's what you choose to be for him. I'll save some money. When this is over, I can find a small house for us. But not around here."

He clenched his jaw. "What does that mean?"

"A lot of rich ladies would have to drape their bodies in my fabrics before I could afford a house in this town."

"Oh," he muttered on an exhale. "This is nothing. You should have seen the house I grew up in. That neighbourhood was filthy rich. This one is only slightly dirty."

Although his tone was light, she heard an underlying trace of resentment. She had never known anyone to complain about being rich.

"Where was that?"

"Outside of Dallas."

"Dallas?" She hadn't detected a hint of a Texas accent in any of the family. "What happened to that house?"

A flicker of emotion flashed in his eyes, or perhaps the light was playing tricks on her. She couldn't be sure. "My brother managed to lose it, along with most of the family inheritance."

"Erik?" she squeaked out.

"No, my older brother, Garret."

Caitlin couldn't hide her surprise. No one had mentioned another brother. Of course, her own family denied her existence, too. "I didn't realize you had an older brother."

His eyes were hooded in sadness. "He died about four years ago in a car accident. He'd read somewhere that an Italian sports car could go two hundred miles an hour, and he decided to test it out."

"I'm sorry."

Andrew shook his head. "He died the way he lived. Too fast, too drunk, and taking stupid chances."

"Did he gamble? Is that what happened to the money?"

"In a manner of speaking. I was over twenty-one when my father passed away, so I received my inheritance and started my company. Garret was the trustee of Erik and Leslie's shares."

The baby began to squirm in his arms, and Andrew forced himself to relax, but his eyes still shone with resentment.

"He got involved with a conniving little con artist. She steered him into a sure thing investment deal that went bust. There was damned little left after his death. She made a fortune in kickbacks while my family had little more than the house left, which was too big and expensive to run."

Caitlin's body went numb. She knew she could never tell him the truth about her past. He would never believe her.

"We sold the house and divided the money between Erik, Leslie, and Mother. Erik used his share to buy into my company. Mother and Leslie came to live with me and used their shares to establish themselves with the country club set."

Andrew paused to take a deep breath. Maybe the past didn't excuse his behaviour, but it might help Caitlin understand why he had been suspicious of her and Maggie.

"Andrew?"

"Yes?" He shook his head and focused on Caitlin, standing above him. Her expression was impossible to read. Was that sadness or fear he saw in the depths of her eyes?

"I have to feed Ty and get him to bed."

"Oh. Sorry."

He held Tyler up. "Here you go, sport. Mommy wants to feed you. Yeah, I'd smile too, if I were you."

A pink flush washed over her. "Give him to me," she muttered.

"Stay here."

Caitlin hesitated.

Andrew could almost read her thoughts. She didn't want to be feeding the baby when Leslie and Joyce returned. Considering their attitude at dinner, he didn't blame her. "They won't be home before midnight. You can bank on that."

"All right. But I'm going to have trouble keeping Tyler awake. You've got him hypnotized."

She sat on the sofa next to Andrew and opened her blouse before taking Tyler in her arms.

Andrew leaned closer. As his bare arm brushed against hers, she trembled. She inched away to break contact.

"Put your shirt on."

"Why?" he asked innocent.

She arched a delicate eyebrow in warning. "Put it on or I'm going upstairs."

"Do I bother you, Caitlin?"

"Yes."

At least she was honest. Her heart might hate him, but her body reacted to the closeness with the same potent excitement that had drawn them together to begin with.

He chuckled. "Good. Despite your words to the contrary, all your memories of that night weren't bad."

"It wasn't the night, Andrew. It was the morning after."

He shook his head. She was not going to give him a break. "Will you ever get beyond that?"

"I don't know."

Andrew reached for his shirt. He slipped his arms through the sleeves but didn't button it. "Better?"

She rolled her eyes and sighed at his deliberate attempt to tease her.

"Erik and Maggie are coming by tomorrow," he said.

Her face lit up. Finally, a smile of pure joy. "Great. I'll finally get to meet Erik."

"You've never met? But he talks about you as if you have."

"We used to speak on the phone every month when I was in Singapore. I was supposed to meet him last week at the house for dinner, but someone served me with a subpoena and I had to leave."

"I didn't mean to ruin your dinner."

"Just my life?"

He exhaled deeply. "Caitlin . . .

"It was a joke, Andrew. Lighten up." She finished feeding the baby in silence. As soon as Tyler fell asleep, she handed him to Andrew. With her clothing back in place, she rose.

"I'm going to turn in myself. I'm tired."

Andrew stood, cradling Tyler to his chest with one arm. Before she could stop him, he lowered his head and brushed his mouth over her pouting lips. A small gasp of surprise was quieted by the kiss. She tasted sweet, stirring memories of their night together. He stroked his hand along her cheek, but made no attempt to draw her closer with the baby between them. Like a fawn caught in the headlights, she seemed stunned into immobility. Her breath quickened, warming his face.

"Good night, Caitlin."

She shook her head and staggered back as if she had just been released from an invisible restraint. When she regained her composure, she glared angrily. "Don't do that again."

"You didn't like the kiss?"

"Yes, I did. So don't do it again."

She spun on her heel and started to leave. When she reached the door, she turned back, gestured irritably toward her son, and waited for Andrew to hand her the baby.

Once she disappeared down the hall, he erupted into laughter. He had gotten her so flustered she had blurted out the truth. Perhaps there was hope after all.

Chapter Six

Caitlin settled into the redwood lawn chair with Tyler squirming in her lap. She took a sip of iced tea, savouring the lingering taste of mint as the morning sun bathed her in warmth.

"So do you like living in the Sinclair mansion?" Maggie asked as she plopped down in a lounge chair with her daughter squealing happily in her arms.

Caitlin wrinkled her nose. "About as much as you did."

Her sister shot her a sympathetic smile. "Got quite a welcome, huh?"

"Oh, yeah. They went out of their way to make me feel at home."

She glanced at her son resting against her bent knees. If she didn't remind herself that this arrangement was in his best interests, she would lose her sanity. When she remembered the way she had let Andrew kiss her last night, she wondered if she already had lost it.

"What about Drew?" Maggie asked.

"What about him?"

"How are the two of you getting along?"

Caitlin raised her hand to shield her eyes from the sun. "I haven't killed him yet."

"But?" Maggie prompted.

"He's the most stubborn, arrogant man on earth. Everything has to be his way. He turned back my car to the leasing company without asking me. And then . . ."

Tyler began to fidget as Caitlin's voice rose. She ran a calming hand over his stomach, then lowered her voice to a soothing whisper. "He leased a Volvo for me. A Volvo. It's bigger than my first apartment. He knows I can't afford the payments, so he tells me that he's paying. Now he's got something he can hold over me."

"Maybe he was trying to be nice."

Nice? Poor deluded Maggie was still caught up in the fantasy. She honestly believed that this arrangement would lead to a declaration of undying love.

"Why would he want to be nice to me?"

"He wants you to see he's not the same man he was last year."

"But he is, except when it comes to Tyler," she admitted somewhat grudgingly.

He fawned over the baby, showing a tender side of himself she wouldn't have believed he possessed. She shook her head violently to clear the kind thoughts of Andrew.

"Otherwise, he's a pigheaded, pushy, unyielding thorn in my side."

Maggie giggled. "Sounds like someone I know well."

"Erik?"

"No. You."

"Me?" Caitlin asked in disbelief. "I think the fact that I'm here proves I'm not stubborn."

"Sure. And he only had to serve you with papers to get you to talk to him, when we both know you've got it bad for the man. Why else would you have had his baby?"

Caitlin stared at her smirking sister. She opened her mouth to deny the charge, but clamped it shut again when she saw the Sinclair brothers heading across the lawn. She waved innocently as they strode into the pool house.

* * * *

Andrew grinned and waved back. So Caitlin was complaining to her sister about him. He had seen the guilty glint in her eyes. Well, if she was talking about him, it must mean she felt something. Since she went to such lengths to appear indifferent, he wasn't sure where he stood with her. On those rare moments when she let her guard down, he had a chance to reach her. Unfortunately, those times were few and far between.

"Does Caitlin like living at the house?" Erik asked as he closed the door behind them.

"Sure, as much as Maggie did."

"Mother and Leslie went all out, I guess."

"Oh, yeah. They went all out."

Andrew grabbed his swimming trunks from the closet and slammed the door. The tense atmosphere in the house was not helping his cause. Last night he thought he had made progress, but by this morning, with the family gathered around, Caitlin had reverted to her wary self.

"How's Caitlin dealing with the situation?"

"She hasn't buried a knife in my back yet."

"Well, that's something, I guess," Erik said dryly.

"Not much. She won't give me an inch. Everything's an argument. I was trying to help her out, so I leased her a car to use. Does she appreciate it?"

"Let me guess—"

"No, she doesn't," Andrew continued. "She bites my head off. Like she really wanted to drive around in that tin box she had! She behaves as if I have an ulterior motive for everything I do."

"Maybe she wants to maintain her independence from you."

"Why?"

Erik cast him a dubious glance. "Because you've never given her a reason to trust you."

"She won't give me a chance. Except when it comes to Tyler."

Andrew thought about how she had left him alone with his son for his own good. She obviously believed his relationship with his son was important, even if she refused to admit it.

"Well, what did you expect?"

"A little more effort on her part. I've bent over backward to be accommodating."

Erik's jaw dropped. "Serving a woman with a subpoena is most accommodating, Drew. Threatening to take away her son is really bending over backward."

"Refusing to answer my calls is reasonable? Not

67

letting me see my son is fair?"

"This isn't about your son, and you know it. You could have come to an arrangement without moving them here. This is about you wanting time with Caitlin."

Yes, damn it, he wanted time with her. He wanted to make up for the past. He wanted to prove he wasn't the man she'd met last year. Hell, he just plain wanted her. Having her in the house, being so close, while she erected an emotional barrier was torture.

"Is that so bad?"

"Not the sentiment, just the way you went about it. If she's only here because she feels threatened by you, what have you won?"

Andrew didn't answer.

* * * *

Caitlin watched Andrew's approach with more interest than was healthy in her present circumstances. The warmth rippling through her body had nothing to do with the sun and everything to do with the view. Royal blue bathing trunks moulded his lean, muscular body. His hair shone like copper in the sun. As he came to a halt in front of her, he grinned with the arrogant self-confidence of a man who knew he was being admired.

"I'll take him for a dip." He reached down and lifted Tyler from her lap.

"Don't be surprised if he shrieks like a banshee. He hates the water."

"Maybe with you. Not with me."

Caitlin pulled a face. "One day and already he thinks he's a mother."

"Speaking of mothers . . ." Erik said as he joined them. "Did Maggie tell you . . ."

Maggie frantically waved her hands to cut her husband off, but Caitlin caught her in the act. She pushed her sunglasses up on her head to better read her sister's expression.

"What's going on?" Caitlin asked.

68

"Nothing."

"It's not nothing."

Maggie shot Erik a thanks-a-lot glare, and then shook her head. "Mom called last night. Sissy's getting married."

"Why were you afraid to mention that? I'm happy for her. Who's she marrying?"

"Quinton Fletcher."

Caitlin almost fell out of the chair with laughter. "Daddy finally landed the banker's son for one of his daughters! He must be over the moon. Why would you think I'd care?"

Maggie's eyes brimmed with moisture. "Because they invited me to the wedding."

Caitlin felt as if she'd been sucker punched, but the smile never left her face. "That's great. You're going, aren't you?"

"You wouldn't mind?"

"Don't be silly." Caitlin slipped her sunglasses back onto the bridge of her nose. "I don't expect you to choose."

A part of her wished Maggie had refused out of principle. Yet it wasn't fair to blame her sister for wanting to be on good terms with everyone. Caitlin clenched her fists and took a deep breath. Envy was a useless emotion. Why upset herself over something she couldn't change? If her parents wanted reconciliation with their oldest daughter, they knew where to find her.

"Is that right, Caitlin?" Andrew's words broke into her thoughts.

Caitlin's eyes focused. Andrew was standing in the pool, beads of water streaming down the expanse of his tanned chest. Her breath caught in her throat. He was, without a doubt, the most gorgeous man she'd ever known. And the most dangerous. She shook her head.

"What did you say?"

"I was telling Andrew how you used to get kicked out of all the stores because you'd go in there to sketch pictures of the dresses, then go home and make an exact copy."

She had forgotten those days. They seemed like a lifetime ago. "That's true. They hung my picture by the cash register. The Copycat Burglar—the most notorious teenager in Greenbrier County."

"Greenbrier County? Where's that?" Andrew asked.

Although his question seemed innocent, Caitlin sensed more than just idle curiosity. If he was so interested in where they came from, why hadn't he asked Maggie? "Another planet."

"Oh, don't listen to her, Andrew. West Virginia isn't even the other side of the country," Maggie supplied happily.

"What part of West Virginia?" Andrew asked.

Beneath his boyish grin, he was pumping Maggie for information. Why? Short of putting a cork in her sister's mouth, Caitlin had no way of preventing Maggie from spilling all their wonderful childhood stories—the sort of anecdotes you share with a spouse or partner, not an adversary.

"Do you plan to turn your son into a lobster?" Caitlin asked, hoping to change the subject.

He glided Tyler across the surface of the water. The baby squealed in delight.

"You're slipping, Caitlin. You referred to him as my son. Who knows what that might lead to? Civil conversations. Parent- teacher nights together."

He made her sound like a vindictive, unreasonable witch and himself the poor, suffering victim. What kind of game was he playing now? "Maybe if you're not otherwise engaged, I'll allow you to escort me to his wedding," she snapped back.

"Children, children, let's not fight over the toy," Erik chided.

Feeling put in her place, Caitlin bowed her head. "You're right, but please don't keep him in the sun too much longer." She turned to her sister. "What should we do about lunch?"

"You know what I could go for?"

"Peanut butter and marshmallow," they said in unison.

"Not you, too," Erik groaned, horrified. "That's all she wanted when she was pregnant"

70

"Me too. But it wasn't easy to come by in Singapore." Caitlin relaxed as she remembered her year away.

"My landlord, Kiki liked to think she spoke English, but I have my doubts. I'd ask for peanut butter and marshmallow and she'd return with an egg roll. If I wanted rocky road ice cream, she'd returned with an egg roll. Ask for an egg roll and I got raw fish. She drove me crazy. I used to accuse her of being on the Sinclair payroll."

"So you thought about me while you were gone," Andrew said smugly.

She crinkled her nose. "Sure I did. Every time I had morning sickness, you were the first person who came to mind."

"They're at it again," Erik grumbled. "I'll bet they couldn't spend more than ten minutes alone without a nasty snipe."

"Put money on it and Caitlin will," Maggie said. "She'd rather pick the fleas off a mad dog than turn down a bet. It's a fatal flaw in her character. She can't refuse a dare and she hates to lose."

"Is that true?" Erik asked.

Caitlin nodded. "Yeah, it's true."

"Then I'll wager one hundred dollars that you can't go one week without insulting him."

"Why me? Why not him, too?" she asked, shooting a pointed glare in Andrew's direction.

"I don't pick fights with you," Andrew said. "I just defend myself."

That was true enough. He never started an argument, but he sure could finish one. "One week, one hundred dollars?" She thought over the offer. "He'll be at work all week. How hard could it be? You're on, Erik. And I'd like the money in crisp new one-dollar bills."

"You haven't won yet. And by the way, little sister- in-law, I've never gone a week without taking a shot at him myself, and he's my brother."

Caitlin lifted her chin. "Around Andrew, I will be the very model of self-control."

She deserved the laughter of the others. If she had

shown one ounce of self-control last year, she wouldn't be in this situation. But she was a year older and infinitely wiser. She gazed at Tyler, smiling and babbling in his father's arms. No, she would not fall for Andrew's brand of charm again, because she had infinitely more to lose.

* * * *

The visit with Maggie and Erik had passed too quickly for Caitlin, especially since she had a long week ahead of her once Andrew returned to work. The excitement of the day had exhausted Tyler, so Caitlin put him down for the night early. She wasn't tired, but with Joyce and Leslie home for the evening, she figured she was safer retiring as well.

The boxes that the car-rental company had returned were stacked in the corner of the nursery. She had put off unpacking, but it was time to accept reality. She was stuck here, at least for the next few months.

Once Tyler's clothes were folded and put away, she crossed through the connecting door to her own room. She sat on the edge of the four-poster bed and pulled the tape off the one box she knew she should ignore.

Inside were mementos of another life. On the top, a green satin hair ribbon she had worn to her first dance was wrapped around a stack of handmade birthday cards from her family. The ticket stub from the theatre where her father had taken her on her tenth birthday jutted out from a worn playbill. A river of emotions ran through her. She closed her eyes and exhaled slowly.

After a pause to collect herself, she continued emptying the box. The smell of flowers in springtime clung to her old softball shirt, which had a pack of potpourri in the pocket. A sad smile tugged at her lips. Every homemade gift, every faded program from school recitals had been preserved and packed with care. She leaned against the bedpost and flipped through a cloth-covered scrapbook. Her chest constricted at the sight of the newspaper clipping announcing her win at the fashion competition. Some memories were better left buried.

From the bottom of the box she pulled out a framed picture. The family photograph had been taken the night she graduated high school. She embraced the picture in a hug, and lay down on the bed. How young she had been back then. And how happy.

* * * *

Andrew stepped inside Tyler's room and stood by the crib. He hadn't started out as the best father in the world, but he intended to make up for his shortcomings. At least his son gave him a chance. Caitlin was another matter.

He glanced though the connecting door to the small adjoining room where Caitlin had curled up on the bed. Her delicate features were bathed in moonlight. Just the sight of her, looking as she had their first night together, caused his hormones to run wild. In sleep, she shed the cloak of wariness she wore in his presence. Would she ever feel that comfortable around him again? In the last year, he had thought about her often. Ironically, now that she was living in his house she seemed beyond his reach.

He walked over to the bed and eased the photograph from her clenched fingers. So Caitlin had not been completely honest when she claimed she didn't need her family. He set the picture on the bedside table and pulled a blanket across her. Could he hope that she had been less than honest when she said she didn't need him, either?

* * * *

Caitlin quickly learned that the best way to handle Andrew's mother was to avoid her. In the five days she had been in the house, Joyce hadn't looked at her grandson once or even referred to him by name. Caitlin was looking forward to returning to work tomorrow, just to escape the tension. Until then, she found solace in the many lakes and parks around the area. She and Tyler left each morning after Andrew and returned home each afternoon at six.

She had to credit Andrew with being a devoted father. After dinner, he spent all his free time with them. For

Andrew, too, Tyler seemed to be a refuge from the tension. Only once did she suggest that she return to her apartment, but Andrew adamantly refused.

Caitlin gathered together a batch of fabric swatches and placed them in a briefcase to give to her boss.

"What are you doing?" Andrew asked as he joined her in the living room. He put the carrier on the coffee table and checked to see that Tyler was still asleep.

"I have to go to the city tomorrow."

"Business?"

"Yes." She flipped the locks on the case and then set it on the floor. "How do I get to the George Washington Bridge?"

He lowered his large frame into the plush sofa with lazy ease. "I'll drive you."

"How will I get back?"

"I'll pick you up or you can meet me at my office."

Her first thought was to decline. Why spend more time with him than she had to? Because you enjoy his company, her conscience mocked her.

He had already won over Tyler. If she were honest with herself, which admittedly wasn't often these days, she felt a small twinge of jealousy at the affection he showed their son. She craved intimacy for herself, as well. Her emotions had become a mass of contradictions. One minute she wanted Andrew; the next she wanted him to keep his distance.

What she really wanted was the control that seemed to be slowly slipping away.

* * * *

Andrew watched the play of emotions on her face and figured she would refuse his offer. She didn't willingly seek out his company. He wished now that she wasn't involved in that silly bet with his brother. He preferred her sarcasm to silence.

"All right," she said.

"You want me to drive you?"

"I don't much care for fighting city traffic anyway. Will you leave my name at the front desk? I don't want another showdown with your security guard."

"They already have orders that you can enter at any time."

An odd surge of pleasure ran through him. She had merely consented to let him battle rush-hour traffic, yet he felt as if a major hurdle had been jumped. He hit the remote control for the television and switched on the evening news. After straightening a blanket over Tyler, Caitlin sat on the sofa near Andrew.

Inching closer, he narrowed the distance between them. He grinned and half expected her to land an elbow in his side. When she didn't assault him, he decided to see how far he could push his luck. He stretched his arms, resting them on the back of the sofa. Every few seconds, he slipped his arm down a few centimetres.

Her emerald eyes sparked with amusement. "For goodness sake, Andrew, any teenager at the drive-in has more finesse than you."

She grabbed his wrist and pulled his arm onto her back. Since her arrival she hadn't initiated intentional contact with him. On the contrary, she had gone out of her way to keep her distance. Never a man to let an opportunity pass him by, Andrew cupped his fingers over her shoulder and drew her closer. As he stroked his hand along her back and arm, she let out a soft sigh. He was reminded of another time she had sighed with pleasure.

Although her warm body rested against his, he felt the tightness in her. She closed her eyes, but she wouldn't give up her wariness of him. He realized that their night together had been very special to Caitlin. Her anger was too strong, her pain too deep. If he had bothered to look, he would have seen the signs that night. No one, not even he, could give that much to another person and walk away unaffected.

If he could get her to acknowledge what she had felt for him, he could move forward, perhaps even rekindle some of those feelings she had buried under a mountain of distrust. Not an easy task, he knew, but the fact that she was with him now, snuggling against him by choice and not by force, meant she wasn't as unreachable as she had led him to believe.

"What's on your mind?" she asked.

He shook his head and focused on her face. "May I ask you something?"

She nodded.

"Why did you stay with me that night?"

Her body went rigid. "It's a little late to start analyzing my motives."

"I'd like an answer all the same." He stroked her silky curtain of hair.

"Why?" She raised her shoulders in a shrug. For a long moment, she said nothing, as if deciding whether or not to answer. When she finally spoke, her words were soft, but filled with emotion. "Because somewhere between half a bottle of champagne and the cold stranger I woke up with was this funny, charming, sweet man who magically took away the loneliness."

"Were you lonely, Caitlin? You didn't seem like someone who would lack for friends."

"Friends aren't the same. The physical contact isn't there. I spent nine years isolated from my family. No one to talk with, to hold me when I hurt. My calls were disconnected and my letters went unanswered. When Maggie finally contacted me, I was going to back out of the contract in Singapore. She begged me not to pass up the opportunity, since she was getting married."

He traced a finger along the side of her face. "You were hurt the other day when she told you about your sister's wedding, weren't you?"

She shook her head. "No. I'm happy for Sissy."

"I meant about your parents inviting Maggie to the wedding."

Caitlin squeezed her eyes shut. "Yeah, it hurt. It hurt a lot. I don't understand . . ."

"What don't you understand?"

"Don't ever make Tyler suffer for choosing to live his own life. If you love him, make sure it's unconditional." Tears were rolling down her cheeks, and she turned her head to wipe them away.

"I would never do that to Tyler."

His words had no effect. Why should he expect them to? He had done nothing to inspire her trust.

"Tyler?" she said, as if she had suddenly heard a noise.

"Is sleeping like a baby, if you'll forgive the pun."

Her gaze darted around the room until it rested on Tyler's carrier. He was sleeping soundly. She relaxed and blinked her eyes against the glow of the brass lamp.

What had happened? For ten years she had buried the pain and resentment and built a good life for herself. She had not shed a single tear for what she had lost. One week in Andrew's house and she had become a spineless wimp. If she didn't pull herself together, she would give Andrew even more ammunition to use against her.

"I'm sorry," she said coolly. She removed his restrictive arm and backed away from him.

"Right back to square one, huh, Caitlin?"

"I don't know what you mean."

His face changed to a grim mask. "For a few moments you forgot I was the enemy and you opened up to me. And that scared the hell out of you, didn't it?"

Chapter Seven

Caitlin looked at Andrew in disbelief. His ego was bigger than his bank account. "You think I'm afraid of you?" She was afraid, but not in the way he meant.

"Yes, I do. I think you're afraid of what will happen between us if you let go of all that anger."

"You couldn't be more wrong." She stood and tried to pass in front of him.

"Am I?" He pulled her down into his lap. The swift movement caught her by surprise and she twisted sideways, grabbing his shoulders for balance. Two steel arms anchored her firmly against his chest.

"Cut it out, Andrew." She squirmed to free herself, but that only made her achingly aware of every muscle of his body, including one she didn't want to notice.

"You're not afraid, are you?"

Oh, he was smug! "Don't be ridiculous."

"Then relax."

Was that what he wanted? To prove she couldn't resist him? That he could get a reaction from her any time he wanted? She'd play his game. Andrew Sinclair was far from irresistible.

She went limp in his arms. "Go on. It's your move."

"That would be too easy. I'm willing to work for it."

He shifted her slightly, fitting her between his hip and the arm of the sofa. He lifted her legs across his lap so that she was reclining.

"Oh, good. The late movie."

"What do you think you're doing?"

"Watching television."

She recognized his strategy. Lull her into a false sense of security and the minute she let down her guard, bam, he

78

would pounce. As long as she remained alert, he wouldn't get the chance. After all, she wasn't the least bit attracted to him any longer.

Liar, her conscience taunted back.

Okay, she might feel a heated attraction to him, but she was also smart enough to keep her distance from a fire so she wouldn't get burned. Caitlin gave her full attention to the television with a steely determination to thwart any attempt to seduce her.

Unfortunately, the film was Hitchcock's masterpiece *The Birds*, and at the first scary moment she buried her head against Andrew's chest. He rubbed his palm over her back and shoulders, drawing her tighter in his embrace. When the eerie music subsided, she found her position had shifted to her disadvantage.

Andrew's warm breath caressed her neck and sent a delightful tingle down her spine. Too stubborn to move away and admit he was right, she did her best to ignore him.

"Are you enjoying the movie?" His eyes never strayed from the television—though his hand glided slowly over her bare leg.

The husky quality of his voice and the closeness from which he asked the innocent question sent an electric jolt to her system. No one should have that much effect over another person with so little effort. In her heart, she was furious with him, but reminding herself of that had no effect on her body.

He ran his finger along the hem of her shorts, grazing her thigh. She drew her knees together to fight against the heat rising in her lower abdomen.

"How long are we going to play this little game, Andrew?" She meant to sound indifferent, bored. He chuckled and she knew she hadn't pulled it off.

"I guess we've played long enough."

He gazed into her gorgeous green eyes, sparkling like emeralds. He felt her try to push him away, only to back down. She wanted that human contact she had spoken of earlier. Someone to hold her, to take away the hurt. What

79

she obviously didn't want was to acknowledge that he could be that person.

He lowered his head until they were inches apart. Warm breath mingled. Their lips met, barely touching. His pulse rate accelerated. She pressed her palms against his shoulders, but as he started to withdraw, she caught his bottom lip between her teeth.

His mouth curved up in a smile, before he covered hers in a deep kiss that forced her lips apart. He pushed his tongue inside her mouth, tasting, teasing, remembering. Everything about her was just as he recalled—the delicate curves of her body, the velvety warmth of her skin, the soft sighs and moans that she could no more suppress than deny.

Caitlin didn't know the meaning of halfway. Once she started, she gave everything—more than he could handle, in light of the circumstances. Tyler was less than ten feet away, blissfully unaware of the sudden rise in temperature. Joyce and Leslie were due home any minute. Not the perfect time to be starting something he definitely wanted to finish.

He cupped her face in his hands. He continued to kiss her, but with less intensity. She pulled back to catch a quick breath. Before she could continue, he lowered her against the arm of the sofa and sat back.

She laughed. "Who's afraid of whom, Andrew?"

"Don't laugh at me."

"Why not? You're funny. You never want what you get."

He gazed down at her amused expression. "I never get what I want, either."

"And what did you want?"

"I wanted Tyler to be tucked in for the night and my mother and sister away for the weekend before I got such an encouraging response from you."

"That's the problem with you spoiled rich guys. You want everything and you don't want to wait."

"I didn't notice you fighting me off."

"I was just playing the game."

"Liar." He slipped his hand under her T-shirt and cupped her full breast. His thumb grazed her taut nipple. Her eyes widened and she let out a startled gasp. "Just playing the game?"

"I'm very sensitive there since Tyler was born." She pushed his hand back.

He arched his eyebrow. "Even before that, I seem to remember."

She ignored his taunt. "May I get up now? I want to put Ty to bed."

"Running away?"

"I prefer to call it a tactical retreat to regroup."

He laughed at her honesty. And her warning. The next time, and there would be a next time, he would be starting over, not picking up where they left off. She wasn't afraid of him. She was afraid of herself.

* * * *

Caitlin came down to breakfast in a grey tailored business suit and white silk blouse. Her hair was pulled into a French braid, secured in the back with a large black bow. Tyler, resting on her hip, tried his best to remove the buttons from her jacket. The aroma of fresh coffee lured her into the dining room.

She wasn't sure who was more surprised by her professional appearance, Andrew or his very hung- over sister. Leslie was nasty enough when sober. Caitlin cringed at the vicious scowl she received when she sat at the table.

"Let me guess. Daddy is taking the little prince into the office to show him off to the peasants," Leslie spat out sarcastically.

"Good morning to you, too," Caitlin said cheerfully. She settled Tyler on her knee and gave him a rattle to keep him occupied. "And to answer your question, I'm taking him to work with me."

Leslie's jaw sagged. "You work?"

Andrew let out a grunt of disgust. "It's not such a novel concept. Not everyone considers polishing off a

81

bottle of scotch a hard day's work."

"Gin, honey. If you're going to be obnoxious, at least get the facts right."

He scowled. "Don't brag about it."

Leslie tossed her hands up in the air. "Hey, we all have to excel at something."

Caitlin couldn't help but feel sorry for Leslie. Her life was so shallow and miserable that she tried to bring everyone down to her level.

"You know, Leslie, I'll bet you could excel at other things if you put your mind to it," she said.

"Oh, sure. Like being a mommy, perhaps?"

Caitlin shook her head. "I was thinking more like modeling. You've got the right temperament and the looks."

"What would you know about it?"

"I worked in modeling for six years. If you ever decide you want to do something with your life, I could introduce you to some people."

"You're going to help me?" Leslie mocked. "No, thanks."

"Your choice," Caitlin said simply.

Despite her words to the contrary, Leslie seemed to be giving the matter serious thought. Her eyes sparkled with interest even though her features remained schooled. She started to say something when Andrew's angry words cut her off.

"At the rate she's drinking, she'll look too old to model before she learns how."

Caitlin groaned inwardly. If Leslie had thought to accept the offer, his mocking comment had stopped her dead.

Leslie stood up and raised her chin defiantly. "Speaking of old, Andrew, thirty-six is a little old to be knocking up your girlfriend, don't you think?" Head held high, she waltzed from the room.

The veins in Andrew's neck bulged. His face turned red, and he looked as if he might breathe fire. "Leslie!"

As he rose to his feet, Caitlin clamped her fingers

around his arm. "Leave her alone. You asked for that one."

"What do you mean, I asked for that?"

"Couldn't you see that she was thinking seriously about accepting? She's never done anything with her life. While she was building up the courage to ask, you shot her right down."

"That didn't give her the right to insult you."

Caitlin shrugged as if it were no big deal. "She didn't insult me. She insulted you. Let it drop, and maybe in a few days she'll swallow her pride and ask again."

He straightened and glanced toward Tyler, gurgling and smiling. There was nothing like a baby to put things in perspective. "You really think she'd be good at something like that?"

"Sure. She's willful, egotistical, and she doesn't take garbage from anyone—all the qualities she needs to claw her way to the top. It worked for you, didn't it?"

"That's a backhanded compliment if ever I heard one."

Caitlin grinned proudly. "We all have to excel at something. Are you finished eating?"

"Yes."

"Would you mind holding Tyler while I have my breakfast?"

"For you? Anything," he whispered seductively. He took Tyler into his arms.

Her eyes widened hopefully. "Anything? Can I move back to my apartment?"

"Anything but that."

"I thought not. Eventually I'll wear you down."

"No, you won't, because you still haven't figured out what it is I want from you."

No, she hadn't figured that out yet. She thought he wanted Tyler and only took her because they came as a set, but his relationship with her was separate and apart from his relationship with his son. What did he want from her? Did she want to know? Was she ready to know?

* * * *

Caitlin hung her briefcase and the diaper bag on the back of the stroller and maneuvered in the front door. She had refused help from Andrew, insisting she could manage on her own. In the past year, she had not painted a flattering portrait of him to her boss and she didn't want him meeting Andrew until she had a chance to explain why she was now living in his house.

Despite the closeness she felt toward Marc, she had never told him about her past. She couldn't explain that she was being threatened without admitting to the source of her fear.

She entered the office to an onslaught of oohs and has. In less than ten seconds, she was relieved of the task of entertaining her son as her coworkers passed Tyler around. With a few minutes' reprieve, she stepped into Marc's office.

"It's about time you showed your face." Marc drew his bushy brows together in a disapproving scowl.

She laughed, and he was unable to contain his own chuckle.

"What happened? Didn't you like the apartment?"

She sat down in the wooden chair across from his desk and sighed. "It was perfect."

"Then why did you leave?"

Caitlin straightened her skirt and launched into her overly rehearsed speech. "Tyler's father decided it would be best for all concerned if we stayed in his house for a while."

"Tyler's father?" Marc's voice was mildly amused.

"Yes, well . . . when I returned from Singapore, Andrew came to see me. He wanted to pursue a relationship with his son, so I decided it would be in Tyler's best interests to go along." She smiled weakly. She wasn't pulling this off.

"So, naturally, being open-minded, liberated parents, you decided to live together in the same house while each maintaining your own lives?"

"Naturally," Caitlin agreed.

"Correct me if I'm wrong. Tyler's father is the same man you once referred to as the stealth bomber, right?"

Caitlin felt the blood rise to her cheeks and she

lowered her head. Comes in under the cover of darkness, drops its bomb and disappears, leaving a mass of destruction in its wake. Yep, she'd said that.

Marc knew her too well to be fooled by her feeble story. "What's he got on you, Caitlin?"

She averted her gaze. Thinking about the past, remembering all she had lost, only rubbed salt into a wound that had never healed. She wanted to let go of the hurt and the anger, but she didn't know how.

"Talk to me," Marc said in a soft, encouraging voice. "I might be able to help you."

"You can't." Her words came out in a whisper of regret.

"Let me be the judge."

Marc had done a lot for her, more than an employee deserved from a boss. She owed him some kind of explanation. Taking a deep breath for courage, she met his questioning stare. "Andrew was going to take me to court for custody. That was his idea of a compromise."

Marc waved his hand in the air as if the idea were absurd. "The most risqué thing you've ever done was lingerie spread for Sears. What could you possibly be afraid of?"

"I guess that really depends on how far back he's willing to dig."

He came around to the front of the desk and put a comforting hand on her shoulder. "You make it sound as if you were a teenage Ma Barker or something."

She shrugged. "If you ask my father, he'd probably tell you I was worse."

"What did you do?"

Caitlin blinked. "That's the sad part. I didn't do anything, except get mixed up with the wrong man at the wrong time. When I won that fashion contest, my father was adamantly opposed to the idea of my leaving. He had a husband all picked out for me. I figured the best way out of the situation was to make sure the guy didn't want to marry me."

"Hardly the crime of the century," Marc said.

85

"There was a new guy in town. An investment broker who was hired by the local bank, fresh from Wall Street with marvellous plans for the town of Weldon. Quinton, my supposed fiancé, touted him all over town as the next Donald Trump. He filled the townsfolk's heads with delusions of grandeur. With just a few thousand dollars invested, they would be millionaires overnight."

Caitlin paused for a breath. "When he asked me on a date, I said yes. He was a conceited bore and downright crude for a supposedly educated man, but I kept seeing him because word got around fast. I figured if Quinton wasn't interested in me any longer, my father would relent and let me study in New York."

Marc tapped his finger against the tip of her nose. "I still don't see what crime you committed. Andrew Sinclair could hardly take you to court for dating a moron when you were eighteen."

If only that man had been a moron. He was a cunning fox who had outsmarted the greedy hounds, and, like hounds, the people wanted blood.

"You have to understand the mountain mentality. To most people a couple thousand is a life's savings. Here comes this apparently wealthy man promising the people they will be living the life they see on television if they trust him with their money, and trust him they did—all except my father. There's a saying that you can't cheat an honest man, and my father was honest to a fault.

"I was so caught up in my own dreams that I didn't see what was going on around me. When I got nowhere trying to reason with my father, I just decided to pack my bag and leave. The same night, Mr. Wall Street skipped out with the life's savings of half the town."

A flash of understanding crossed his face. "Let me guess. They thought you were involved in the scam?"

"Involved? They figured I had planned it with the guy. They needed someone to blame, rather than admit a smooth-talking stranger had conned them out of their money without help, especially since my father was one of the few who didn't lose money."

"Were you ever charged with anything?"

"It doesn't matter. My own father thought I was involved. Can you imagine what a good lawyer could do with something like that?"

"Probably nothing, Caitlin. It was ten years ago. There are mothers who commit murder and don't lose custody of their children."

"Not if their father is a millionaire who wants his son. When you come up against a man with money who will do anything to win, the truth never enters into it anymore. Tyler is the most important person in my life, and I would rather die than lose him. As long as I play by Andrew's rules for a while, I don't have to take the risk."

Marc gazed at her sympathetically. He was as close to her as her own father had once been and had looked after her in much the same way. "How do you know he won't try to take him later on?"

"He promised. And no matter what his other faults may be, I don't think he'll break his word. I only have to stay until Tyler is old enough to be on his own for a day at a time."

"I'm not sure what kind of advice I could give you. I guess there's nothing I wouldn't do to protect one of my kids. I suppose it won't kill you to live with him a few months."

"No, it won't kill me." In fact, she was coming to enjoy his company more than she ought to. "Should we get to work? My son will want lunch soon."

He looked as if he wanted to add something, then bowed his head in agreement. "All right. But before we do, Casey has one of her special requests. She wants you to make this."

He handed her a picture. Marc's 14-year-old daughter was a major clothes horse. Whenever a hot singer introduced a new look, she begged Caitlin to make her a replica. The Copycat Burglar would strike again.

87

Chapter Eight

"Andrew. Are you with me?" Erik's voice broke the silence in the room.

Andrew glanced down at the reports on his desk and tried to concentrate. Business was the farthest thing from his mind.

"Sorry. I'm preoccupied."

"Problems with Caitlin?"

His tone suggested where he thought the real problem lay. Andrew knew Maggie and Erik considered him unreasonable, but he couldn't back down. Tyler was awake for precious few hours. Commuting to Connecticut would cut into that time, and he doubted Caitlin would allow him to sleep at her apartment.

Then there was Caitlin herself. He refused to admit to jealousy, an emotion he'd always found useless, but he felt better knowing she was under his roof each night. As it was, he had no idea where she spent her days. How could he ask? He had told her she was free to come and go as she pleased.

"Yo, Drew Are you on this planet?"

He glanced at his smirking brother. "No. No problems with Caitlin. She's adjusting better than Mother and Leslie."

"What did you expect? You know how they treated Maggie when we were married."

"I didn't expect a miracle, but Mother hasn't looked at my son once. He's my son, for God's sake. Why are they making me choose?"

"They'll come around," Erik said with little conviction.

"Leslie might, if she ever gets herself out of a bottle long enough. It's frightening. She's Garret all over again."

Erik stiffened at the mention of their older brother.

"That's a bit extreme."

Andrew sighed. No one talked about Garret. No one admitted he'd had a problem. Maybe that's why Leslie had learned nothing from his death. He rubbed his temples and reached in his desk for his blood-pressure medication. He swallowed the tablets with a sip of water and got back to the reports on his desk. Making himself sick wouldn't change a thing.

* * * *

As the elevator doors opened, Caitlin tried to quell the churning in her stomach. She should have let Andrew pick her up as he'd suggested. Her last visit to Sinclair Electronics was one that she—and half the office staff—remembered all too vividly.

This time, however, Andrew had clearly left very specific orders. She was greeted with a smile and an immediate call to Andrew to announce her arrival.

He met her at the front desk and lifted Tyler from her arms. "You're early."

"He's adorable, sir," the receptionist said. "A relative?"

"Yes. He's my son."

The woman's jaw dropped, a response repeated by others as Andrew introduced his son to his staff. However, in his obviously proud moment, he seemed to have forgotten her name. Although unintentional on Andrew's part, he was making Caitlin feel like a fool.

By the time they reached his office, Caitlin wanted to smack the silly grin from his face, but when she saw Erik, she suppressed the urge.

"You're awfully quiet. What's wrong?" Andrew asked her.

"Hello, Erik," she said, ignoring his question.

Erik, obviously more astute than his older brother, placed a quick kiss on her cheek and headed for the door. "I think I'd better leave before the explosion."

"No. Finish what you were doing." She settled in a seat

in the corner of the room.

"We were finished," Erik assured her and left.

Andrew sat in the chair across from her. "You want to tell me what I did this time?"

"All right, since you asked. It might have been nice if you had introduced me, too. My name is not Tyler's Mother. You made it sound like I was a breeder who popped out a baby for you."

"You're being ridiculous."

"Am I?" She lowered her head. "How would you feel if I introduced you to the people I work with as 'Tyler's father,' as if you were some kind of afterthought?"

"I probably wouldn't like it," he conceded. "But how was I supposed to introduce you? As my former lover? You would've slugged me. I'm sorry," he said, his voice growing softer, "I'm not sure what I am in your life, Caitlin, but you're too damned frustrating to be an afterthought in mine."

Caitlin felt a little of the anger subside. Maybe she had overreacted. What were they to one another? The question sent her stomach fluttering. She was developing strong feelings for Andrew, or rather rediscovering the feelings that had drawn her to him in the first place. Despite the threat to her emotional well-being, her heart had decided to ignore all the good advice of her logical mind.

She found a small comfort in the fact that she was frustrating him. At least it worked both ways. "The problem is, you're too used to getting your own way," she said, trying to get the conversation back on her terms.

"If I always got my own way, we'd be in bed right now," he shot back.

Her cheeks flushed hot. "I can't believe you said that in front of your child."

Andrew lifted Tyler above his head. "What do you think, sport? Does it shock you to know I find your mother incredibly sexy?"

"Stop it," she muttered.

"Why? I'm having a man-to-man talk with my son. Don't you think your mother's beautiful?" He turned the baby toward Caitlin. Tyler gurgled happily. "See, he agrees."

"I doubt he's got the same thing in mind as you."

Andrew's gaze rested on the cleavage exposed by the deep cut of her silk blouse. "No? We both want to be in the same place right now."

She held her head high and grinned. "Maybe. But Tyler has a better chance than you."

"That sounds like a challenge. What would you say to an early dinner? Do you feel like oysters?"

Caitlin almost had to laugh. He was coming at her like a steamroller. When Andrew turned on the charm, he was infinitely dangerous.

"Try a little subtlety, Andrew. Like Spanish Fly."

"Have you got any?"

"I give up." She threw her hands in the air. In a war of words, she would not win. He flashed her a smile of triumph and she quickly amended her statement. "For the time being."

"I never thought otherwise."

* * * *

Rather than going to a restaurant, Caitlin suggested they pick up sandwiches and go to a park near the house. Andrew didn't even know the place existed. In the eight years he had resided in New Jersey, the roads to and from the office were the only ones he'd traveled. How much of life had passed by him unnoticed?

Caitlin tossed her jacket in the car and pulled her blouse free from her skirt So much for the cool businesswoman. She looked more like an eccentric artist. After setting the food on a picnic table, she waded barefoot into the stream and dipped Tyler's toes in the water. When he'd had enough, she put him in the stroller and joined Andrew at the table.

She handed Andrew a sandwich from the paper bag. He removed the wax paper and lifted the top slice of bread. "This one's yours."

"They're both the same."

"I asked for mayo and salt."

"And I ignored you. If you want to commit suicide, be my guest, but don't expect me to hand you the ammunition. You're on medication for high blood pressure."

He smiled. "Why are you so worried about my health?"

"Because you're of no use to your son dead."

"He'd be a rich little boy," he joked.

Caitlin apparently failed to see the humor. "If I wanted your money, I would have sued you for it. You're getting enough aggravation in your life right now. Don't compound the problem."

Her impassioned words surprised him. "I can't figure you. You claim to care nothing for me, yet you get in a snit over my dietary habits."

"Snit? You're picking up your vocabulary from Maggie. Just because I think you're an overbearing, pigheaded skunk doesn't mean I don't care what happens to you."

"Why, thank you," he chuckled. "That was touching, Caitlin."

"I'd like your relationship with Tyler to be long-lasting. I mean, really, would you rather have salt on your sandwich or an extra day with your son?"

"Okay, you're right."

The corners of her mouth lifted in a grin. "I always am."

"Not always. I'm not pigheaded. You are."

"Me?" she squeaked out. "How can you say that?"

"It has something to do with your unwavering distrust of me. Can't we forget about last year and start over?"

She glanced at Tyler. "It's kind of hard to forget when I have a little twelve-pound replica of you staring me in the face every day."

"All the more reason for us to try to work things out between us," he said.

"And you think that's possible, given our history?"

"It might help if you'd let go of some of your anger."

She shook her head. "I can't. It's how I survive. How I've always survived."

"Perhaps the answer is to begin with your family. If you went to see them—"

"No." Her reply was swift and adamant.

She missed her family, he was sure. Why did she become visibly agitated at the thought of visiting them? Her colour had paled, and she refused to meet his gaze. She twisted the napkin in her fingers until it shredded from the tension.

Something had happened back in West Virginia that stopped Caitlin from returning home, and it was more than a broken engagement. His mind reeled with the possibilities. She was terrified of someone or something— so much so that she had agreed to all his demands rather than chance his finding out.

She wasn't angry with him, she was afraid of him. Why hadn't he seen it sooner?

He became even more determined to discover the truth. What he had done to her was rotten. He knew that. But they would never be able to move forward while she was haunted by the past. He had enough to make up for with his own sins. He didn't need to be paying for someone else's as well.

If he couldn't get answers from her, he had one other hope. "Would you like to go visit Maggie and Erik this weekend? We could leave after work tomorrow."

"Really? Maybe they have plans already." Her eyes brightened with excitement. The lift in her spirits would make the trip worthwhile, even if he learned nothing.

"If they want to go out, I'm sure we can find a way to entertain ourselves."

She didn't raise an eyebrow at the suggestive tone in his voice. "I'll have the clothes packed and ready by six."

He chuckled. "If I know you, you'll go home and pack tonight."

"Ah, but you don't know me. I leave everything until the last minute. That way I won't be disappointed if the plans fall through. Besides, I haven't figured out where the laundry room is yet. I have clothes to wash."

Andrew swallowed the last bite of his sandwich. "We don't pay a maid to watch you do your laundry."

She smiled gently. "Sally has enough work to do teaching you how to take Tyler out of his carrier."

He looked away. "She told you?"

"I asked her to keep an eye on you."

"You didn't think I could handle him?"

"Be honest. You didn't think you could handle him. I'd never seen anyone look more scared than you did when I walked out that door. But what a treat to find Mr. Macho changing a diaper when I returned."

"You didn't know I was the strong, silent, sensitive type."

She let out a whoop. She was laughing at him, but he didn't care. For once the tears that filled her eyes were caused by amusement rather than hurt.

"Strong, yes. Silent, never. And sensitive? In your dreams, maybe."

"I'm insulted."

She pressed her hand against his chest and absently ran her finger along the jacket lapel. "Oh, loosen up. You're such a stuffed shirt." She seemed unaware of the impact her touch had on him.

"What do you suggest? Should I kick off my shoes and go wading in the stream?"

"It's a start. Lose the tie while you're at it."

He draped the red paisley tie around her neck and kicked off his leather shoes. He tossed his jacket onto the picnic bench and swept her up in his arms before she could lodge a protest. In four quick steps he was dangling her over the water's edge. She locked her arms around his neck in a choke hold.

"Don't you dare."

"Loosen up, Caitlin—although I happen to like the way your shirt is stuffed."

"Put me down," she demanded.

"Give me some incentive," he said, staring into her eyes.

She expelled a deep sigh. Ignoring every warning she'd given him, every barrier she'd erected, he continued to try to break through her defences. But as difficult as it was to fight him, fighting herself was damned near impossible.

She kissed him.

As he deepened the kiss, he lowered her legs to the ground. Their bodies moulded together. A warm tingling began in her belly and spread like wildfire through her. His masculine scent was heady, evoking memories she had tried hard to forget. He felt too good to resist, and the worst part was he knew it. Alarm bells sounded in her mind, but she didn't heed the warning. Her purely physical reactions allowed her to forget. She didn't need to think, only react to the powerful sensations running through her.

His hand slipped boldly under her blouse, caressing her flesh with strong, fluid strokes. One last shred of sanity told her to stop him, but he ran his fingers into her hair and pulled her head closer. He nipped playfully at her ear, coaxing a response she couldn't suppress. She knew this was a bad idea, but his raw sexuality was more than she could fight.

As he continued his sweet assault on her senses, she had neither the will nor the desire to end the kiss.

Andrew was the first to draw back. She let out a soft sigh of protest before realizing just what she had done. Embarrassment brought a warm flush to her cheeks. This was not what she needed in her life right now. Losing her heart to Andrew again could be dangerous.

Did he know how much he affected her?

One glance at him and she knew the answer. His triumphant smile was more than she could take. Leaning down by the bank of the stream, she cupped her hands into the water and repeatedly splashed it over him. As he reached for her, she darted under his outstretched hand and ran to the stroller, lifting Tyler into her arms. Andrew wouldn't retaliate while she was holding the baby.

He raked his fingers through his damp hair. "I'll get you eventually."

His wet shirt clung to his chest, defining the well-toned muscles beneath. An overwhelming urge to stroke her hands over his body brought a shudder of longing. That's keeping cool, calm, and detached, she chided herself.

He caught her staring and grinned again. "Let's go home."

"Maybe you should dry off a bit first. If your mother sees you like that, she'll accuse me of trying to make a peasant out of you."

"Then that will be my revenge."

* * * *

Andrew's revenge was sweet.

Joyce apparently wasn't expecting them back so early, as she had a guest in the living room. "Was there some kind of accident?" she asked icily, eyeing Andrew's disheveled appearance.

"No." He nodded to the visitor. "Hello, Mrs. Forsythe."

Caitlin wanted to crawl into the nearest hole and disappear. Mrs. Forsythe glared down her long nose at the sight before her. Her perfectly coiffed and lacquered hair didn't move as she turned to Joyce for an introduction.

Joyce shot Caitlin a hateful scowl that chilled her to the marrow. "This is Ms. Adams, Erik's sister-in- law."

Andrew went rigid. He took Tyler from Caitlin's arms and held him up. At least his mother had finally seen him, if in fact she could see anything through her blazing eyes.

"And this is our son, Tyler," Andrew added.

Mrs. Forsythe gasped.

Joyce groaned.

Caitlin cringed.

The only one not at a loss for words was Andrew.

"If you'll excuse us, ladies, we have to get changed."

He slipped a possessive arm across Caitlin's back and led her away.

She was going to make sure she wasn't alone with

Joyce any time in the near future, Caitlin thought. Andrew was playing a dangerous game of nerves with his mother, and she was the pawn. If she couldn't get him to call a halt, she might have more to worry about than resisting Andrew. Joyce had nothing to lose and everything to gain by getting rid of Caitlin and Tyler.

* * * *

Leslie entered the salon, intent on getting herself a drink. She would need it to make it through the evening with her mother. Joyce was storming through the house like a tornado taking down anything in its path.

She opened the cabinets of the bar and came up empty. Her hand started to shake. Damn! What was happening? Panic washed over her. For a fleeting moment, she wondered if she had a drinking problem, then quickly dismissed the notion. The only problem she had was her arrogant brother and his insistence on keeping that woman in the house.

"Looking for something?" Andrew asked.

Leslie whirled around. Judging by his cynical smirk, she'd bet he was the one who had emptied the liquor cabinet

"Well, if it isn't Father of the Year. Where's the little mother? Out on a shopping binge?"

"Better than a drinking binge," he shot back.

"It must be you, Drew. All the women in your life feel the need to go out on some kind of binge."

His eyes narrowed and she thought she saw a flash of sorrow. "You're only hurting yourself, Leslie."

She didn't want or need pity from Mr. High and Mighty. "You, on the other hand, aim for the whole family."

He folded his arms across his chest. "Meaning?"

"It's obvious you brought her here to embarrass us. I hope you're happy about the way you humiliated your own mother by parading your bimbo—"

With an angry wave of the hand, he cut her off. "If you

have a problem with me, go ahead and get it off your chest. But leave Caitlin out of this."

"Sure. The woman is ruining our family, but we're not allowed to talk about her."

"Don't blame her for our problems, Leslie."

She rolled her eyes and continued her search. She found a small bottle of gin hidden behind the seltzer and raised it triumphantly in the air.

"You missed one."

"If you want to drink yourself into a stupor, I can't stop you."

"You've got that right," she said defiantly. "You can't stop me from doing anything."

"I know." He snatched the bottle from her hand. "But keep in mind I don't have to pay for your habits, either."

He left the room before she could come up with a suitable retort. How dare he? He'd never given a damn about her—or anyone else, for that matter.

Her mother was right. They had a serious problem. Caitlin Adams had given Andrew more than a son. She had given him a freaking conscience. There was nothing more obnoxious than a reformed rake.

Chapter Nine

The morning sun filtered through the lace curtains, casting a doily pattern on the wall. Caitlin stretched her arms above her head and yawned. The last remnants of sleep clung to her like a warm blanket. The carriage clock on the nightstand chimed eight times. How had she slept so late? Tyler was usually up by six o'clock.

She jumped out of bed and grabbed her robe. Tyler wasn't in the portable crib she had set up in Allison's room the night before. With a sign of relief, she realized that Maggie must have taken both babies down to allow her sister to sleep in.

After changing into her cutoff shorts and an oversized T-shirt, Caitlin headed downstairs. Maggie was in the kitchen, washing dishes, while the two cousins rolled around in the playpen.

"About time you got up," Maggie joked.

Caitlin smiled. "I know. I haven't slept this late in four months. I'm surprised he's not screaming for his breakfast"

Maggie handed her a cup of coffee and joined her at the table. "I hope you don't mind. I gave him a bottle."

"That's fine." Caitlin took a gulp of the strong brew, hoping to zap her tired body to life. "I hope we didn't wake you last night when we arrived. The traffic was awful and we got here so late."

"You'll have to forgive my lack of manners. I heard you on the intercom when you set up the crib, but I was too comfortable to move."

"I don't blame you. If I had a handsome husband keeping me warm, I wouldn't get up, either."

Maggie arched an eyebrow. "Oh, yeah? You know, it's not necessary to use both guest rooms."

Caitlin let out an exaggerated groan. "Does your misguided matchmaking ever cease?"

"That depends. Did you lose your bet, or does Erik owe you a hundred dollars?"

"If you don't count when I called him a pigheaded skunk or when I told him that a teenager at the drive-in had more finesse than he did, I won."

"Sounds like there's a good story behind that one," Erik called out from the living room.

Caitlin lowered her head as the colour flooded her cheeks. "Why didn't you tell me he was up?"

"He and Andrew have been up for a while."

"Andrew, too? Oh, no." She leaned back in her chair to peer through the archway at the two laughing faces and grumbled a good morning to them. "Only eight o'clock and already my foot is in my mouth."

"Your foot is always in your mouth. The hour of the day has nothing to do with it," Maggie said.

Although Caitlin couldn't argue with the truth, she still kicked her sister playfully in the leg. She did have an uncanny talent for speaking first and listening afterwards.

Erik appeared in the doorway. "So, Caitlin, tell me why you said my big brother has no finesse," he urged.

She took another sip of her coffee. "It's a long story."

"I've got nothing better to do this morning. Come on. I'm going for a jog up the beach and these two lazy bums aren't interested in moving. I'll race you."

"You're on," she cheerfully agreed. A good brisk run would get her adrenaline pumping. If not, at least it would keep her out of trouble.

* * * *

Andrew stared out the window and watched Caitlin and Erik race along the beach. He felt a stab of jealousy toward his own brother. Why couldn't she relax like that around him?

He was grateful, however, for the opportunity to speak with Maggie alone. Time was running out. His mother and sister were making life a living hell, and he wasn't sure how much longer Caitlin would be willing to put up with it. He needed answers about her past before they could go forward.

He joined Maggie for a cup of coffee at the kitchen table. "Do you like living on Long Island?" he began tentatively.

"Yes."

"It gets crowded in the summer."

"I suppose."

That was the extent of his ability to engage in small talk. Patience and tact were two virtues he'd never felt the need to cultivate. During a long silence, they both stared into their mugs.

"There's something I wanted . . ." they said in unison, then stopped and laughed.

"You first," Andrew said.

Maggie toyed with the edge of a napkin. "I think that you and Caitlin have gotten closer. At least that's the impression I got."

He grinned. If Caitlin's sister had that impression, then maybe he really was making progress.

"I'd like to think we have."

"I got a letter from my sister, Sissy. You have to understand. Sissy is a bit tactless and selfish. She wanted me to ask Caitlin to make her wedding dress from a picture she found in a magazine. I don't know if I should mention it to Caitlin."

Andrew slammed his cup down on the table, sending a swish of dark liquid over the rim. His first instinct was to call the unfeeling bitch and give her hell. How could anyone have the nerve to make a request like that after ten years of silence, particularly for a wedding she didn't have the decency to invite her sister to?

On second thought, he decided, this might be the icebreaker she needed. Surely her family couldn't ask that of Caitlin and still ignore her existence.

"Are they going to invite her to the wedding?" he asked.

Maggie frowned and shook her head sadly. "No. Sissy didn't tell my father. She plans to say I sent the dress."

"What happened, Maggie? Why is there all this animosity toward Caitlin? And why is she so afraid I'll find out?"

She recoiled as if the words had been a slap. "I can't answer that."

"But you know, don't you?"

"I can't tell you," she said. "I'm sorry."

"I don't want to hurt her."

She raised her head and met his stare. "Three weeks ago you were willing to take her to court for custody. I don't imagine there's a more hurtful thing you could do to her."

"Is that what she's afraid of? Does she think that if I find out what happened I'll use it against her in court? Did she do something—"?"

"She didn't do anything!" Maggie's angry outburst gave him more information than she had intended to reveal.

He placed his hand over hers and spoke softly. "But they think she did, right?"

Maggie looked away. "I can't tell you, Drew. I promised."

"All right. I'll wait until she's ready to tell me on her own. I don't know what advice I could give you about the dress. She might want to do it for her sister. On the other hand, she's very hurt by the silence. She's not quite as tough as she acts."

"I know. That's why I didn't want Erik to say anything. Now I'm in a pickle."

He let out a bitter laugh. Now there was a word to describe Caitlin's life—sealed in a vacuum, left to ferment in bitter juices, and no way out unless someone opened the lid.

* * * *

Caitlin did her best to keep up with Erik. They jogged for about a mile along the shore before her stamina gave out. She doubled over with her hands on her knees to catch her breath. Her toes sank in the wet sand as waves lapped against the shore.

She glanced up to find Erik laughing at her. "What's so funny?"

"You've got my brother tied up in knots."

She struggled to regain her breathing. "And that amuses you?"

"Oh, yes. Serving you with custody papers was unforgivable. What I can't figure out is why you forgave him."

She straightened and pushed her hair back from her face. "Who says I have?"

His eyes danced in the morning sun. "You're just like your sister. Neither one of you can hide what you feel. If there wasn't something there, you would have been on the first plane back to Singapore."

"I considered it."

"But you couldn't. Did you ever ask yourself why?"

Only a hundred times a day. She had told herself that Tyler was the reason, but that wasn't true.

"I don't know. There's something about Andrew. He can be so—" Sexy. Tempting. Exciting. For once she kept her thoughts to herself. "—charming when he wants to be." He had charmed the pants off her, both figuratively and literally.

"So what's the problem?"

"Your mother, for starters."

His face clouded over with regret. "I know she's been giving you a hard time."

"That's not the problem. She gives Andrew a hard time. His blood pressure skyrockets every time he has a conversation with her."

"Mother doesn't converse, she lectures," Erik corrected with a trace of humor.

"Yes, well, as you know, Andrew doesn't sit by idly and get lectured. He lashes out. And you know who she's going to blame in the end? Me."

"Talk to Andrew."

103

"Then he can get a double dose of aggravation. That will really help his blood pressure. He can't threaten your mother and sister into accepting me, and I don't want to put him in a position where he has to choose."

Erik lifted his shoulders helplessly. "I've tried to convince him to let you move back into the apartment. He won't listen. He believes his son should be in his house."

"I know. But if he won't back down, then I wish he would back off. I don't want him to get hurt—or to get caught in the cross fire myself."

"I'll talk to him, but to tell you the truth, he'd take it better coming from you. He lashes out because he thinks Mother is hurting you. She hasn't changed. He has."

"What do you mean?"

"Our mother has always been cold and undemonstrative. Before he met you, Andrew used to be just like her. I know he has an odd way of showing it, but he cares about you and Tyler."

"Well, you're half right. He cares about Tyler."

"And you as well, Caitlin." Erik placed his thumb under her chin and tilted her head up. "And I think you feel the same. Maybe in time, when the hurt and the anger fade, you'll even be able to admit it."

* * * *

After covering herself with a generous dose of sunblock, Caitlin stretched out in a beach chair next to her sister and turned her face up to the sun. Tyler and Allison were soon asleep on the blanket underneath a huge umbrella, lulled by the gentle lapping of the waves against the shore. For ten minutes, she enjoyed the blessed silence, until she realized that Maggie was never silent for that long.

"What's eatin' you, Margaret?"

"Oh, God, no one's called me that in ages." Maggie grinned. "Remember how Sean used to call me The Shadow because I followed the two of you everywhere?"

At the mention of her brother, Caitlin felt a hollow

ache in her chest. Sean had been more than her brother, he had been her best friend. She reached in her bag for her sunglasses and slipped them on. A weekend that had started with such high expectations had quickly become an emotional fiasco.

"Does it bother you if I talk about the family, Caitlin?"

"No. Of course not," she lied. "Have you heard any news recently?"

"Well, I got a letter from Sissy yesterday."

"That's nice. How is she?"

Maggie shrugged. "You know what she's like. Expects everyone to go all out because she's marrying into the Fletcher family."

"And she's welcome to them. I suppose she expects a big gift from you."

"She might have gone too far," Maggie muttered.

Her sister rarely spoke with anger about anyone. Maggie had even forgiven Andrew, so the resentment in her voice surprised Caitlin.

"What do you mean?"

"Promise me you won't get upset."

"About what?"

"Sissy wanted me to ask you to make her wedding dress. The one she picked out costs seventeen hundred dollars, and she thought you could make a copy." Maggie's words tumbled out with breathless anxiety. "I'd understand if you said no."

Well, give the girl points for audacity, Caitlin thought, willing away the tears that sprang to her eyes. Still, Sissy was her sister and years ago Caitlin had promised to make her wedding dress. She kept her promises, even when the rest of the family had forgotten theirs. For hadn't they promised to love each other forever?

"Tell her I'll do it," she choked out.

"I shouldn't have told you. Me and my big mouth," Maggie groaned.

"I'm glad you did. It will be a pleasure to help marry her off to Quinton Fletcher. Besides, it will give me something to do this week. I can go to the design centre and use the large cutting tables. It's the perfect excuse to avoid Joyce."

"Joyce can be a witch."

Caitlin would have chosen a more appropriate rhyming word. She changed the subject. "Do you and Erik have plans tonight? Maybe we can con Andrew into taking us out to dinner."

Maggie's smile returned, broad and knowing. "It wouldn't take much conning. He'd agree to anything you ask."

"Anything but moving back to her apartment," Andrew's voice grumbled from behind. Maggie reddened, but Caitlin was undisturbed.

"People who eavesdrop on private conversations never hear anything good about themselves," she tossed over her shoulder.

"Not your conversations, anyway." Andrew sat on the corner of the blanket next to her and handed her the bottle of suntan oil. "Would you do my back, honey?"

Caitlin bristled. Honey? Had he actually called her honey? What was next, Sweetie? She took the cap off the bottle and held it firmly in her grasp. Placing her free hand on his back, she urged him forward. His triumphant grin faded as she pulled back the elastic waistband and squirted half the bottle of oil down the back of his swimming trunks.

"Don't you ever call me honey again!"

Andrew straightened. Maggie's barely suppressed giggles and Caitlin's outright snicker sent the blood straight to his face.

"You vindictive little brat."

He came to his feet and hoisted Caitlin out of her chair. Effortlessly he carried her waist deep into the water and tossed her in. She came to the surface laughing even harder.

"I hate it when you laugh at me," he growled.

"I know. That's why I do it."

He dunked her under the water and held her for a few seconds. When she came up for air coughing and sputtering, he was stricken with guilt. He hadn't meant to hurt her, only teach her a lesson.

"I'm so sorry." He pulled her into his arms and patted her back until she stopped coughing. "Are you all right?"

She gazed up at him—and broke out in a wide grin. "Gotcha."

Another wave of anger washed over him. No one else could stir such wrath in him—or such desire. He ran his hands over her back, then down her arms to cup her elbows. "Damn it," he said softly, "you scared me."

"Serves you right I don't like to be called honey or sugar or any other nickname that makes me sound like some treat for a man. My name is Caitlin."

"Point made. We're even now. Let's go back to shore before I get in any more trouble."

But neither of them moved.

He pushed back a strand of hair from her face and grazed a kiss over her cheek.

The water beat rhythmically against their bodies. Caitlin closed her eyes and, with a soft sigh, let her body relax against his. The lazy ups and downs of the ocean as he held her close wreaked havoc on his body.

Caitlin got to him in a way no woman had before. With just one look, one small touch, she unleashed a fire in him that smoldered for hours. He slid his hands to the narrow indentation of her waist. With his elbows, he urged her arms up around his neck. A breeze danced over them.

* * * *

Caitlin trembled until his mouth came down on hers. Then the shivers running through her were a different kind altogether. She returned the kiss with an urgency that matched his. She wanted him as much as he seemed to want her. How a man could have that kind of physical reaction while standing in the cold Atlantic Ocean was beyond her.

More surprising was the way he managed to ignite a raging inferno in her. She had never been able to resist him, and she wasn't sure she wanted to anymore. The feel of his lips on hers, the taste of him, obliterated all rational thought from her mind. She was very close to losing control and way beyond caring.

A loud wolf-whistle broke the intimate mood. Long Island in the middle of the summer was not an ideal place to indulge in a necking session. As a group of teenagers applauded their public display, Caitlin wriggled free from his embrace and slipped under the water.

"Did that cool you off?" Andrew asked.

"Not a bit." Before he could reach for her again, she dove under the water and swam to shore. As she dragged herself up the beach, tired out from the strong currents, she turned back to catch a glimpse of Andrew's face. He looked like the Cheshire cat, mighty pleased with himself. She joined Maggie and was treated to another knowing smile.

"Shut up," Caitlin warned.

"Good thing you're not interested. I'd hate to see what you might have done out there if you were."

She threw herself down on the blanket with a grunt. "I admit it, I'm spineless! Can I help it if his touch turns my legs to Jell-O and my brains to spaghetti?"

"Why don't you tell him and put the man out of his misery?"

"He already knows. I won't give him the satisfaction of hearing me say it." When she had agreed to Andrew's bargain, the last thing she'd envisioned was falling for him again. Until Andrew trusted her enough to give her back her freedom, she couldn't trust him with her heart.

Chapter Ten

Andrew paused outside the nursery door and watched Caitlin make a fuss over putting Tyler to sleep. She had been quiet and withdrawn ever since this morning on the beach. Had her sister mentioned the wedding dress, or was something else bothering her?

He hated seeing her unhappy, particularly when he had to acknowledge that he was part of the reason. The family life he offered her was not the quaint and cozy Rockwell painting that she had lost. That was something all his money couldn't buy for her.

She turned and half smiled. "Erik and Maggie leave already?"

"Yeah. They said they'd be back around midnight."

"Oh." She lowered her head. "We have to talk, Andrew."

"I know."

They walked together down the hallway. Tension blanketed him like a winter fog. She paused outside her bedroom door. As if to gather her courage, she braced herself against the wall and exhaled slowly.

He tried to come up with a rebuttal to what he was sure would be an argument over her moving back to her apartment. To threaten her now would be a giant step backward in their relationship.

"Look, Caitlin, I know my family has been unbearable, but I'm sure in time . . ." His words trailed off as a believable lie eluded him.

"That's not what's bothering me."

"Then what's wrong?"

"The way you react. You're not helping by going out

of your way to antagonize your mother. She blames me afterward."

He cupped his hands over her shoulders. "Has she done something to you?"

"No. But it's just more unpleasant than it has to be. I can ignore her if you can. This is a temporary arrangement we have. You're still going to have to deal with her long after I'm gone."

A mix of emotions ran through him; disappointment at the reminder that their living arrangement wasn't permanent, and relief that she hadn't insisted on leaving immediately. Never one to push his luck while on a winning streak, he agreed. "I'll try it your way for a while."

She nodded and gave him a grateful smile. "Thank you."

A long silence hung between them, and he felt every bit the awkward teenager she had once jokingly called him. "Do you want to watch television?"

"No. It's all reruns."

He shrugged indifferently, but Caitlin noticed the disappointment on his face. "I guess you're tired," he said.

The smart course of action would have been to say good night and retreat into the room. But when she gazed up at him, her heart stopped listening to her head. She wanted him. Part of her even needed him. But what broke through her defences was the look of longing on his face that allowed her to believe that, just maybe, he needed her too.

"I'm not that tired. I'm up to a few games."

He shook his head violently as if he didn't trust his own hearing. "Excuse me?"

"You seem surprised," she noted with a satisfied smile. "Was that or was that not what you were thinking?"

A glimmer of hope sparkled in his golden eyes. "What kind of games did you have in mind? Cards? Monopoly? Trivial Pursuit?"

She reached for his hands and tugged him into the bedroom. "I'm not sure I'd call you a trivial pursuit. Foolish, possibly. Trivial, never."

"I'm not sure what you're getting at. You're going to have to tell me the rules of this game you want to play."

Caitlin felt her cheeks burn. What had happened to her courage? She could sure use half a bottle of champagne. No, she decided. She wanted nothing to dull her senses. If she was going to regret this later, then she wanted to enjoy every minute now.

She took a deep breath. "The rules? Well, first we take off this." She pulled his polo shirt over his head and tossed it onto a chair.

"And the next rule?"

"I never did much care for rules. I prefer a free- for-all." She tilted her head up and sprinkled a line of kisses along his neck and face. Her finger traced a path down the centre of his torso, twisting at the soft mat of hair on his chest. "Have you figured out the game yet, Andrew?"

He inhaled sharply. "Yeah. It's called Torment Your Opponent."

His mouth lifted in a lazy grin, then brushed over her lips. Before he could take possession, she lowered her head and traced her tongue along the same path her hand had taken. As he reached for her, she sat on the bed and pinned his arms to his sides. She continued to press kisses against his stomach.

One gentle tug on the waistband of his jeans brought him down next to her. With her tongue, she laved the hard tip of his nipple.

He groaned.

She gazed at him and grinned. "You're very sensitive there."

"I think you're cheating," he barely managed to choke out.

"You can't cheat in a free-for-all." She continued her seductive exploration of his body. As she had that first night with him, she closed her mind to anything but the moment. Any consequences she would deal with later. Right now, she needed him. She wanted him. And in truth, she loved him.

With trembling hands, she reached for the snap of his

jeans and tugged them open. She slipped her hand inside, her fingers tangling in the hair below his navel.

"This isn't a game. You're trying to kill me."

His raspy voice, heavy with passion, moved her. Even without his heartfelt words, she knew what she did to him. She continued to arouse him, enjoying her power. In this part of their relationship, she felt equal to him.

"You know, this is a game for two."

This time when he reached for her, she offered no resistance. When he ran his hand over the outside of her shirt, she quivered in anticipation.

"First rule, we get rid of this, right?" he asked. He removed her shirt and tossed it on top of his.

He explored every nuance of her neck and shoulders, covering her skin in moist kisses. Her body swayed and she held onto him for support. 'Jell-O' flashed through her mind; then all coherent thought vanished.

His mouth covered her breast, sucking and releasing the hard peak until she thought she would go mad. It wasn't enough. She wanted more.

Impatiently, she pulled at her remaining clothes with frustration. Andrew covered her hands with one of his own. As if enjoying his revenge, he took his time removing her clothing, thwarting any attempt on her part to hurry the process. Then his own jeans landed in a careless heap on the floor.

She reached for him. He knelt down next to her and parted her legs with his hand. He knew just where to touch her to get a response. Her body writhed as he ran his fingers along the inside of her thigh.

He stroked her cheek with his other hand and pushed back the hair from her face. "Do you like that?"

Heat coursed through her. She opened her mouth to answer, but all that came out was a muttered cry as he moved his hand higher, intimately caressing the folds of skin, damp with desire. Her body shuddered from the pure pleasure he gave her.

"No more games, Andrew."

The plea in her voice was more than he could fight

against. He had a burning need to feel her beneath him again, to be inside her. Nothing before in his life had come close to what he had shared with her.

Some last-minute flash of reality brought him back long enough to fumble for his jeans and extract a foil packet from his wallet. One time was forgivable. Twice would be stupid.

In seconds he was back, lowering himself over her. As he pressed inside, she tensed almost imperceptibly. So attuned to her was he, he noticed immediately and paused to give her time to accommodate him.

"Are you okay now?"

"Never been better." She wrapped her arms and legs tightly around him. As their bodies moved together in an escalating rhythm, it was impossible to tell where he ended and she began. They were one, joined by a white-hot passion that consumed them, and she matched his every move as if she had been made just for him.

The air seemed to explode around them. She whispered his name like a prayer as she gave in to the release, arching her back, as if to meet the tremors that washed over her.

Andrew squeezed his eyes shut in a last-ditch effort to retain his tentative control. As her muscles clenched around him, the last of his control shattered. He thrust deeply inside her one last time and gave into his own long-awaited climax.

When the final shimmering tremors of release ebbed, he collapsed on top of her. She wriggled beneath him until she found a position where her soft curves would absorb the weight of him. When he tried to move, she tightened her hold.

Locking his arm around her waist, he flipped to his back and pulled her on top of him. Long strands of her silky hair fell across his shoulders. She kissed him, then folded her arms on his chest and rested her head on them.

"Are you planning to sleep right there?"

"Have you got a problem with that?"

"None at all. I didn't think you would want me here when your sister got back."

Caitlin raised her head and giggled. "I think she'd be devastated if you weren't. This morning, they had no plans. Then suddenly, out of nowhere, they had a previous engagement."

Andrew slid her down to the bed and cradled her in his arms. "I do like your sister."

"It's amazing what happens when you get to know someone before passing judgment."

He expelled a groan. Was he ever going to get beyond that? "I want to get something straight. I did feel that Erik and Maggie were rushing into marriage too quickly, and I had hoped to talk them out of it. Not because she wasn't good enough, as Maggie believed, but because they had only known each other a month. It wasn't until I met you that I realized it sometimes takes only a minute to know if something is right."

"Then why didn't you tell me who you were when you sat down at my table?"

He grinned devilishly. "Lady, you had me hotter than Texas chili before my ass landed in the chair. You weren't exactly trying to discourage me, either. My brother's marriage was the farthest thing from my mind. I felt so guilty the next morning I was sick."

She playfully punched him in the shoulder. "You sure took it out on me."

"Before I could explain that I had changed my mind, you had called your sister. I had to keep an eye on that letter opener on the desk for fear of what you'd do to me. When you threw that money on the bed, I wished you had buried the thing in my back."

Caitlin smiled. "I thought it was a nice touch, until I discovered that I didn't have the cab fare back to Staten Island. Two subways, one ferry, and a bus ride later, I wished I'd buried something in you, too. Only your back wasn't the part of your anatomy I had in mind."

He winced. "I don't think I could say I'm sorry often enough."

She brushed a lock of hair away from his forehead. "If you gave the matter some thought, I'm sure you could find a way to make me forget."

Andrew cocked his eyebrow in question. "What did you have in mind?"

"Television?" she suggested as she wriggled against him. Her warm skin brushing against his felt like silk.

He turned on his side and gently eased her beneath him. "It's all reruns."

"How about rerunning the last half hour?"

"I think I could manage that."

Her eyes reflected a trace of humor and something more. "I'm sure you can. Stamina was never your problem. But there's something I need to know first."

"What?"

"How hot is Texas chili?"

Andrew chuckled. He used his knee to open her legs. His hips pressed against her and she felt the fullness of his arousal.

"That hot?" she said and sighed.

* * * *

Long after Caitlin had fallen asleep, Andrew remained awake, staring at the ceiling. He should have felt pleased with himself. He didn't. Sex had never been the problem between them.   Why had he expected it to be the answer?

He slid his gaze to her. Silky dark hair spilled over her shoulders and onto his chest. She curled against him, as serene and content as a lifelong lover. He could almost convince himself that forcing his way into her life had been right. Almost. In truth, all he had managed to prove was that she still wanted him physically. She had never denied that.

So what had he expected? A declaration of her undying love? This evening, before inviting him into her room, she had made a point of reminding him their arrangement was temporary.

She couldn't still believe that he would try to take Tyler from her. He didn't care what the hell she had done in the past. The Caitlin he knew was a gentle, loving

115

mother, and the closest thing to heaven he was likely to find on Earth.

Was she with him now because she genuinely cared about him or because she wanted to appease him? He hated this nagging suspicion that she still doubted him.

Chapter Eleven

Caitlin wasn't sorry to get away from Maggie's incessant teasing. Her sister began by serving Jell-O for breakfast Sunday morning, and she didn't let up until Andrew and Caitlin had left for home late in the afternoon.

Monday morning she started work on Sissy's wedding dress. Marc gave her an office to use where she could set up Tyler's playpen while she worked. The dress her sister had chosen had a six-foot train, and the entire bodice had to be hand sewn with tiny faux pearls. Once Caitlin made the pattern for the dress, several sewing machine operators helpfully stitched the garment together for her.

By Wednesday, everything was completed except the hand stitching, which she could do from the house. Because she needed to bring a mannequin home, she asked Andrew to pick her up after work. At four-thirty he breezed into her office, looking devastating in his three-piece suit. Not as good as he looked with nothing at all, she conceded, but her pulse rate quickened just the same. He lifted Tyler from the playpen and sat in the chair across from her desk.

"Are you almost ready?"

"I'm ready. I want to get out of here before my boss gets back," she joked.

"Too late," Marc's amused voice called out from the door.

"Oh, great," she grumbled and glanced between the two men. "Marc Stevens, Andrew Sinclair."

Andrew supported Tyler with one arm and held out his free hand.

"I ought to kill you," Marc said with a laugh, but he shook Andrew's hand.

"What did I do?" Andrew asked.

"Look at her. She had a baby. Now she's too fat to model."

Caitlin let out an indignant snort. The fashion houses liked their models to be rail thin and flat chested, but she rather liked the way she had filled out since Tyler's birth.

Andrew ran a lingering gaze along the length of her. "I think she's perfect."

"I haven't modeled in years, so what's it to you anyway, Marc?"

"You started a trend. Two of my best models decided that their biological clocks were ticking away and they went out and got pregnant without the benefit of husbands. What is it with women? We give you the vote and now you think you don't need us."

She just rolled her eyes. If she'd thought he was serious, she wouldn't have worked with him for ten years. "I might be able to help you out with a model."

"What's she like?" Marc asked.

"Beautiful, willful, and self-centred," Andrew interjected.

"And a natural redhead," Caitlin added.

"She sounds perfect. You know I trust your judgment on that, Caitlin. I have to fly. I have a meeting." As quickly as Marc had entered, he was gone.

Caitlin began to fold the portable playpen.

"Is that why you had Tyler? Because your biological clock was ticking?" Andrew said.

"You shouldn't take anything Marc says too seriously." How could she explain motives she had never tried to analyze herself?

"I'd like to know."

"If the only reason I had Tyler was because I was afraid of getting old, I wouldn't have been much use to him as a mother. I wanted a baby. I was in a position where I could afford to raise a child alone."

He came to his feet, ready for battle. Surprisingly, she didn't feel like arguing with him.

She put her hands above her head in surrender. "I was wrong. But at the time, I figured I would be raising him

118

alone. I can't say what I might have done if I'd been eighteen and pregnant, but my age didn't play a role in my decision to have him. Besides, I'm not old."

Caitlin collected her belongings. When they had everything packed into the car, Andrew came around to the side and opened her door.

"Tick, tick, tick," he joked.

"I don't know why you're so amused. You've still got a few years on me."

"But I can father a child when I'm ninety," he retorted smugly.

"Who'd want you when you're ninety?"

"I bet I could make you want me."

His conceit was remarkable. So what if he was right? She didn't have to feed his inflated ego by agreeing. "I'd be well into my eighties by then and I'd probably get a bigger charge out of my electric blanket."

He laughed. As she settled in the bucket seat, he closed the door and came around the car to slip in behind the wheel. "You know what tonight is, don't you?"

"Family comedy night on television?" she guessed.

"Bridge night. Leslie and Mother will be out. How shall we pass the time?"

Caitlin feigned consternation. "I don't know. Maybe I could cook tonight. I found a fabulous recipe for chili."

"I'll bet you did." He traced his finger along the side of her face and drew her closer for a tender kiss. "Could I convince you to stick around for breakfast?"

"I'm not a big breakfast eater."

"I don't know about that. Sunday morning you seemed to be insatiable."

Damn him! He just had to remind her that she had no willpower and even less self-control when he touched her. Her entire body flushed. She turned and gazed out the window. "Do you plan to spend the night in the parking garage?"

"Another tactical retreat, Caitlin? Aren't we beyond them yet?"

"Better than surrender." Until she knew where she

stood with him, surrender was an option she couldn't afford to exercise.

* * * *

Leslie stumbled down the stairs with a massive headache that refused to subside. The annoying racket of jingling rattles and infant gurgling coming from the studio intensified the throbbing. She shuffled across the parquet floor and paused outside the door.

Caitlin was kneeling on the floor, playing with her son as if she genuinely enjoyed the experience. Leslie tried to picture her own mother doing the same and laughed inwardly.

Then she glanced around the room and caught sight of the satin and lace wedding gown on the mannequin. Her stomach knotted. Andrew couldn't be planning to marry her!

She walked into the studio and let out a grunt. "Do you have to make those disgusting sounds so early in the morning?" she said, although it was after eleven.

Caitlin glanced up. "Good day to you, too," she said cheerfully.

Leslie shot a glance toward Tyler. "Why don't you put clothes on him? Certainly Andrew can afford them."

"I don't take money from your brother, and I can afford them myself. He prefers to be naked," Caitlin said, even though the baby was wearing a diaper. She leaned forward and pressed noisy kisses against Tyler's belly.

"Will you be taking him on your honeymoon?"

"What?"

Leslie lifted her gaze toward the dress. "That is your wedding dress, I assume. Although it's a bit tacky to wear white when you've already anticipated the wedding night."

"It's a wedding dress, but not for me."

"What's the matter? Can't you get him to pop the question?"

"I really don't see what concern that is of yours." Caitlin kept her gaze firmly on her son.

120

"Oh, come on, don't deny you've been dangling your little brat in front of him for a while. You know he'd do anything to get his hands on that kid."

"Letting your vicious tongue out for an airing, Leslie?" Andrew asked sharply.

Both Caitlin and Leslie started.

"I thought you were at work," Caitlin said.

He loosened his tie, which appeared to be choking him. "I had an early meeting in South Jersey, so I took the rest of the day off. It's nice to see my charming sister keeping you company in my absence."

"Hey, I try my best," Leslie said. "Well, I'll leave the two of you to play Mommy and Daddy." She gave a mock salute to Andrew and waltzed out of the room.

"Ignore her," Caitlin said softly, grabbing his wrist as he started to follow.

Despite her indifferent words, Andrew knew the cruel snipes had to hurt. Although he had promised to overlook the deliberate insults from his mother and sister, following through had been difficult. "I don't see how you can."

"It's easy. I don't care. As long as you're home, would you mind taking Ty? I have a few hours left on this dress."

"Sure." He came up behind her and slipped his hands around her waist. Lemon scented hair brushed his cheek.

She giggled and squirmed to free herself. "Cut it out."

After the nasty barbs she'd had to endure from Leslie, he could understand her reluctance. That didn't make it any easier when he had to cool his passions under a cold shower.

He rested his chin on her shoulder and pressed a kiss against her cheek. "The dress is beautiful. Your sister doesn't deserve your talents."

"You're gonna lecture me about doing something for a sister who doesn't deserve it?" He playfully elbowed his ribs. "Go on. Get out of here. I can't concentrate on my work."

Andrew smiled. "Good. That makes two of us." He bent down and scooped Tyler up in his arms.

"Bring him back when he's hungry."

121

"How will I know?"

She laughed. "He'll let you know."

* * * *

With a deep sigh, Caitlin buried her head under the pillow and tried to go back to sleep. She wasn't ready to get up from her nap. Her shoulders still ached from the five hours of work she had done that morning.

Try though she did, sleep eluded her. Something at the edge of her awareness was bothering her. The silence should have been conducive to sleep. The intercom was on. She should hear something, if only the sounds of sleep. She put the receiver to her ear, hoping to hear a familiar noise.

Her legs tangled in the comforter as she jumped from the bed. She kicked free and opened the connecting door to the nursery. Tyler was missing. Her heart raced wildly and a cold chill washed over her. After a few panicked seconds, she remembered that Andrew was home. He must have taken Tyler to allow her to enjoy her nap.

She went to the bathroom to splash some water on her face before heading down to find her son. She heard Andrew's voice coming from the living room, followed by Joyce's shrill one. Although she had no wish to confront Joyce when she was in one of her moods, the atmosphere wasn't healthy for a baby. Taking a deep breath, she entered the room.

Andrew and Joyce looked up.

"I'm sorry," Caitlin told the two scowling faces. "I just came for Ty."

"He's in the nursery," Andrew said.

The air left her body. "No, he's not. I just came from there."

In two steps, Andrew was at her side, grabbing her arms as her legs began to buckle. "He's probably with one of the maids."

"What's all the fuss about?" Joyce asked. "Leslie took him out to the pool."

"What?" both Caitlin and Andrew exclaimed at the

same time.

"You're the one who said we should try to get along, Andrew," Joyce reminded him.

"You let her take a baby out by the pool when you know she's been drinking? Are you out of your mind?"

Caitlin shut her mind to the conversation and glanced out the floor-length windows to the back yard. "Oh, my God."

Andrew followed her terrified stare. Leslie was bouncing up and down on the diving board, with Tyler in her arms. Cursing, Andrew ran out the sliding-glass door.

He was already at the side of the pool when Caitlin caught up to him.

"Leslie," Andrew called out sharply. "Turn around slowly and walk off the diving board."

Leslie laughed maliciously and dangled Tyler over the water. "Behold the only person Andrew Sinclair has ever cared about in his self-centred life."

The pounding in Caitlin's chest deafened her to any sound but Tyler's piercing cries. In a trancelike state, she stepped up onto the diving board.

Leslie spun around and teetered. She pulled Tyler against her chest and took two steps forward to regain her balance.

"Give him to me," Caitlin said, holding her arms out in front of her.

"But we're having so much fun."

Caitlin's fingers clenched into fists and she fought to control her rocky emotions. She couldn't take the chance of angering Leslie any more. "Please, Leslie. He's just a baby."

Pain flashed in Leslie's eyes. She gazed down at Tyler, kicking and screaming in her arms, then squeezed her eyelids together as if trying to shut out the sight. Once she regained control of herself, she raised a malevolent grin toward Andrew.

"You want him, Drew, you come get him."

Andrew's mouth was a thin white slit. He squared his shoulders and stepped on the board. The last threads of his control were slipping and only a pleading gaze from Caitlin kept him from losing what little calm he still possessed. "Hand the baby to Caitlin."

Leslie shook her head. "You know, as soon as he finds a way, he's going to take your son from you."

"Give him to me," Caitlin begged.

"When Andrew says please."

"Please, Leslie," he said quietly.

Leslie grinned triumphantly and took a step forward to hand the baby to Caitlin. "Take your brat." Caitlin clasped Tyler against her chest, stroking his head and whispering to him in an attempt to calm him. His cries lessened from sheer exhaustion, she feared, rather than a feeling of safety.

Andrew came over to check the baby. He reached out to stroke his cheek but she cradled Tyler closer and backed away from him. Her heart rate was beginning to slow, the panic of the last few minutes giving way to angry relief. She had never been so frightened in all her life. What Leslie had done was beyond comprehension and beyond anything she would expose Tyler to again.

"Your sister is deeply troubled," she snapped, and ran past him into the house.

* * * *

Andrew stood motionless at the end of the pool. Although he'd never been a violent man, he honestly thought he was capable of murder right now.

Leslie strolled off the diving board, laughing as she passed him. "I'll bet that scared you, Drew."

It was the last straw. "You nasty little bitch." He caught her wrist and dragged her back to the house.

"You're hurting me," she yelled.

"Not nearly as much as I'd like to," he growled. He crossed the lawn and shoved her though the open doors.

"Andrew, let her go," Joyce demanded.

He paused long enough to send her an icy glare. "As soon as I'm finished, I want to talk to you."

He jerked on Leslie's arm and continued to the

124

bathroom. With little effort, he pushed her into the shower. She huddled against the wall, for the first time looking conscious of the magnitude of his wrath. When he reached inside, her hands went up to protect her head. He flipped on the cold water and slammed the shower door.

Ignoring her shrieks, he said, "When you're sufficiently sober, I'll expect to see you in the living room."

Chapter Twelve

Fifteen minutes later, Leslie joined Andrew and Joyce. She took a seat next to her mother and raised her head rebelliously. Andrew paced for several seconds, then took the seat across from them.

"You win, Les," he began calmly. "You can't seem to live in this house with Caitlin and Tyler, so after today, you won't have to."

"You mean they're leaving?" Joyce exchanged a meaningful glance with Leslie.

Andrew leaned back and regarded them with cold indifference. "You misunderstood. They're not leaving. Leslie is. You have one hour to pack your clothes, and then I want you out of my house. And don't bother trying Erik. He wouldn't let you near his child, either."

Joyce's jaw sagged. "I can't believe that you would turn against your family for that—"

"Don't say it." He looked back and forth between the two in disgust. "You still don't get it, either of you. Tyler is my family. I told you the first day if you made me choose, you would be unhappy."

"You can't be serious. What am I supposed to do?" Leslie asked.

"I don't care. You have your bank account. That should keep you in gin for a few months."

"Andrew!" Joyce cried out.

"What?" Andrew sprang from the chair. He clamped his fingers around Leslie's chin and turned her head toward his mother. "Don't you see what's happened to her, or don't you care? She's Garret all over again. No. She's worse. Garret only killed himself. She almost killed a little baby whose only crime was being my son."

Leslie swatted his hand away. "I wasn't going to hurt him."

"I won't take that chance. You are leaving. If you want to kill yourself, do it without my help."

"You can't do that," Joyce bellowed.

"Oh, yes, I can. And as for you, my loving mother, listen carefully." He towered above her to be sure he had her full attention. "Caitlin and I share a son. That makes her more my family than you or Leslie ever tried to be. To you I'm a chequebook, so let me spell this out in terms you can understand. If you do or say anything to Caitlin that so much as brings a frown to her beautiful face, you can look forward to spending your golden years in a senior citizens' home and living off your Social Security cheque."

Joyce rose from the chair. "You can't mean that."

He smiled. "Try me. I have to go away on business for a few days. When I return, Caitlin and Tyler had better be the two happiest people in all of Ramapo Heights."

* * * *

Caitlin did everything she could to soothe Tyler, but the fright had been too much for him. He wouldn't suckle, so in desperation she tried a bottle; he turned his head and pushed with his tiny fists.

His heartbreaking cries were a torment. She prowled around the room, gently bouncing him, singing every lullaby she could think of. Finally he began to calm down. The quieter Tyler became, the angrier she felt. She had reached her limit. She would take her chances with the court rather than subject her son to that again.

Andrew strode into the nursery. "How is he?"

She turned on him. "How do you think he is? He's been throwing up, he won't eat, and he's exhausted from screaming."

His face twisted in pain. She felt guilty, but she couldn't stop herself from lashing out at somebody.

"Let me hold him," he said softly.

"Leave us alone."

127

"Please, Caitlin. It will never happen again."

"You're damned right it won't. I'm leaving here tonight. Go ahead and sue me if you want."

He shook his head. "That won't be necessary. Leslie is leaving."

Caitlin whirled around, stunned. He had thrown his sister out because of her? "What is she going to do?"

"I don't know and I don't care. I've already watched one member of my family drink himself into an early grave. I won't watch it again."

The pain in Andrew's words cooled her burning anger. She had forgotten about his older brother. How hard it must have been on him. "Perhaps it is better if she has to stand on her own."

She returned her attention to Tyler, who had begun to cry when she stopped jiggling him. But her stiff movements had the opposite effect from what she sought.

"Let me hold him for a while," Andrew said. "You're only making it worse."

"I can take care of my son."

"Right now, you can't take care of yourself. Sit down and let me try."

She shot him an indignant scowl. "Be my guest." Andrew wrapped Tyler in a tender embrace and rubbed his hand in circles on the baby's back.

He hummed a lullaby, the soft vibration of his voice soothing both mother and child. He tucked Tyler's head under his chin and crooned, "Nobody will ever hurt you again."

Caitlin slumped into the rocking chair. She felt a combination of relief and envy at the easy way Andrew instilled a sense of safety in Tyler, so much so that he had managed to put Tyler to sleep when her many attempts had failed miserably.

"Should I put him down in the crib?" he asked.

"You can try."

* * * *

128

Once he'd settled Tyler, Andrew knelt down in front of Caitlin. Convincing his son that everything would be all right had been the easy part. Getting through to Caitlin was another matter.

He tucked an errant strand of hair behind her ear and left his hand resting against her cheek. She eyed him warily, but she didn't pull away.

"I still think it would be better if I left," she whispered.

"No!" His answer was not a demand but a plea. "Two weeks, Caitlin. If things don't improve, you can move wherever you want and I won't take you to court."

"I can't live like this. Your mother will never accept your son. It's making you sick."

"She will accept him, or she will find another place to live."

A silvery tear streamed down her cheek. "This is breaking your family apart. How long will it be before you start to resent me for it?"

"I lost my family long before you entered my life." He brushed a kiss over her lips. The taste of salty tears lingered.

Although she stared straight at him, her expression seemed distant. He couldn't let her withdraw from him, not when he had finally begun to make progress. He leaned closer and touched her arm. Her skin was warm and velvety soft. He moved his hands to her waist and lifted her out of the chair.

She let out a groan of protest and pushed her palms against his chest. Sitting back on his heels, he settled her in his lap and stroked her back, then slid his hands up her sides until they brushed her breasts.

"Andrew, I don't think . . ." Her words trailed off as his mouth covered hers.

If he couldn't calm her down, at least he could try to change the focus of her nervous energy. Kneading the tense muscles of her arms and shoulders brought him a moan of appreciation. Within seconds she surrendered, wrapping her arms around his neck and returning his hungry kiss. She pressed closer, slipping her hand under his shirt and

129

twisting her fingers into the mat of hair on his chest. His stomach muscles bunched. He felt the start of a smile forming on her lips. She enjoyed tormenting him.

"Two weeks, Caitlin?" he whispered against her mouth.

She lifted her head and drew an uneven breath. "That's not fair."

"I know and I'm sorry." But he didn't stop his sensual onslaught. He couldn't afford to be fair. This one last time, he had to win.

With her defences weakened, he had obtained her agreement, but the victory was hollow, for she didn't trust him any more now than she had before.

* * * *

Caitlin packed her bag and was ready to leave by eight o'clock in the morning. When Andrew said he was going away on an unavoidable business trip, she knew she had to get out of the house herself. A visit to Maggie's for a few days would keep her out of Joyce's way.

During breakfast, Andrew seemed unusually quiet and moody. He was probably tired. He had spent the entire night on the floor in the nursery so that Tyler wouldn't be alone if he woke up during the night.

Once Andrew left, Caitlin went to feed and change Tyler for the drive to Long Island. She rocked the chair and hummed softly as he suckled.

"Caitlin?"

Her head shot up. It was the last voice she expected to hear. Leslie stood in the hall outside the nursery. Her arrogance had apparently deserted her. She hovered in the doorway, looking pale and sullen—and, amazingly, sober.

"Haven't you done enough damage?" Caitlin asked angrily.

Leslie slumped her shoulders and averted her gaze. "I wouldn't have hurt him."

Her words sounded sincere, but Caitlin wasn't in a forgiving mood. "Oh, you wouldn't have? Well, you might not have meant any harm, but anything could have happened. You could have killed him."

"I'm sorry."

"I'm sorry doesn't cut it this time. He's four months old. What the hell did he ever do to you to make you hate him so much?"

"It's not Tyler I resent. It's Andrew."

Caitlin snorted. "Andrew? He gives you everything."

"You try living like that," Leslie said bitterly. "I don't want him to give me everything. I wanted to work. He wouldn't give me a job but he gave Erik one."

"Erik went to college and sank his own money into the company so they could expand."

Leslie's eyes rounded in surprise. She genuinely didn't know. "I didn't ask to start as a vice president. He wouldn't even consider an office job."

Caitlin laughed. "You don't know your brother at all, do you?"

"What do you mean?"

"The only way to get anywhere with Andrew is to be more stubborn that he is. If you don't fight, how does he know you really want it?"

"Andrew's pigheaded. He doesn't back down."

How well I know that, Caitlin thought. "You're not helpless, Leslie. If he won't give you a job, then go somewhere else. He's not the only boss in the world."

Leslie stood tall and appeared to be gathering her courage. Or swallowing her pride. "Is that offer about the modeling position still open?"

During the lengthy pause, Leslie fidgeted nervously. Caitlin wasn't sure Leslie deserved her help, but a job would keep her out of trouble. For Andrew's sake, she would help Leslie. If a family could be salvaged, it was always worth the effort.

"It's hard work and it's not glamorous. It could take a long time before you're ever picked for a fashion shoot. Most times you're little more than a human dummy."

"Well, I do excel at that," Leslie said with biting honesty. "I'm really sorry about Tyler. Is he all right?"

Caitlin pressed a kiss to the baby's forehead. "He's a bit jumpy. It will take a while before he's back to normal."

"Will you talk to Andrew for me? Tell him I'm sorry?"

"No. You have to do that yourself," Caitlin said. "But wait a couple of days. Right now he's angrier than I am."

"I know. He threw me out—not that I blame him. My own friends won't take me in."

Caitlin stroked Tyler's cheek to keep him awake a few more minutes. She had a long drive ahead and she hoped he would sleep through most of it.

"You know, Leslie, the doctor told your brother to avoid stress. That didn't help him."

"I didn't know he was sick."

"He's not sick, and I'd like him to stay that way. And another thing. If you want help from me, then I want something from you. You have a drinking problem. Do something before it takes over your life."

"I don't mean any disrespect, but why do you care?"

"Because you're Tyler's aunt. Once I leave here, he'll be visiting on his own. I don't want to be scared to death every time he's with his father."

Leslie regarded her curiously. "You really are leaving?"

"Does that surprise you?"

"Well, yes. The way Andrew talks, I got the impression ... I mean . . . my mother thinks ..."

"Let's not discuss your mother." Caitlin cut her off. "I know what she thinks of me."

"I guess we both made our positions painfully obvious."

More than obvious, Caitlin silently agreed. Perhaps in Leslie's case, there was hope for a change. Once Tyler fell asleep, she lifted him away from her breast and straightened her blouse. "Let's go."

"What?"

"You want a job. My boss needs a model. Let's go before he fills the position."

Leslie glanced down at her powder blue shorts and top. "Shouldn't I change first?"

"Not unless you want him to think you have something unsightly to hide. And a word of advice. Play up the Texan accent you try to hide. Texas beauties are the rage this season."

"You're being very generous under the circumstances."

Caitlin smiled broadly. "No, I'm not. Marc is a tyrant to work for. I'm going to enjoy seeing you sweat."

When they arrived in the city, the design centre was bustling with activity. Photographers were everywhere, preparing a shoot for a mail-order catalogue. Caitlin had a hard time pulling Leslie away. There was a gleam in her eyes that Caitlin had never seen before.

They finally made their way to Marc's office. He gave Caitlin a small hug and tweaked Tyler's nose as he slept in her arms.

"Marc, this is Leslie, the woman I've been telling you about She's here about the modeling position."

"Turn around," he ordered.

Leslie gazed questioningly at Caitlin. She made a circular motion with her finger and Leslie turned a slow pirouette.

"What size is she?" he asked Caitlin, ignoring Leslie's presence.

"Four, I'd guess."

Marc placed his hand under Leslie's chin and turned her head from side to side, studying the perfect angles and contours of her face. "You'd better slow down, kid, or you're gonna age real fast. How much do you weigh?"

"One hundred and two," Leslie barely whispered.

"If you gain one pound, you're out."

"Does that mean I got the job?" she asked hopefully.

Marc nodded and pointed for her to take a seat. He towered over her with a grim expression plastered to his face.

"That means you are expected to be here at eight o'clock and you stay until three whether or not you are needed that day. Any outside jobs have to be done on your own time. If you are lucky enough to be chosen for a catalogue or a showing, you will be here at six a.m. for makeup and hair. I don't care if your brother is some big millionaire. We don't have any princesses here."

Caitlin had to stifle a hoot of laughter. She would bet that no one had ever talked to Leslie Sinclair in that tone of voice. And she just grinned as if Marc were groveling at her feet. While he was reading her the riot act, one of the photographers burst through the door. Marc glanced up and scowled.

"What is it, Anton?"

"We're two hours behind. Where's the damned redhead?" Anton gazed at Leslie and pushed his fingers through her long hair. "Alleluia. A redhead who won't have roots in three weeks. Why isn't she in makeup?"

Leslie gestured helplessly.

"Answer the man," Mark said.

Her eyes rounded in panic. To see the unflappable Miss Sinclair at a loss for words made the trip a success for Caitlin. Leslie wasn't even aware that she had fallen into an opportunity most girls out there would die for.

"Don't look at me." Caitlin said. "If you want to work, you better get your rear end out there before Anton changes his mind. He's a temperamental cuss."

"Are you here to work or aren't you?" Anton grunted at her.

"I don't know what I'm doing," Leslie sputtered out.

"Your job is to look pretty and move when we tell you. It ain't brain surgery, lady."

She raised her head and gathered that Sinclair arrogance Caitlin was so familiar with. "Are you staying?"

Caitlin shook her head. "No. You'll have to find your own way home."

Leslie waltzed out the door without saying goodbye, but for once her lack of manners was forgivable. Caitlin and Marc burst out laughing at the same time.

"I think we scared the hell out of her. But she'll go places if she's ambitious. You always could pick 'em, Caitlin."

"Yeah. I could pick 'em. I just wasn't one of 'em. I

waited two years to get a catalogue shoot myself," she complained.

"Redheaded beauties are hard to come by. I had three dark-haired models back then who wanted it more than you did. That's the nature of the business. And being in the right place at the right time. Some people are born lucky." He grinned and glanced at Tyler, sleeping soundly. "And some get pregnant on the first try."

"That's a cheap shot, even for you."

"How's life with Tyler's daddy?"

Caitlin rose to leave. "You just took care of one of my biggest problems," she said. "Now, she's yours. Revenge is sweet." Caitlin laughed herself silly all the way to the car.

Chapter Thirteen

Andrew sat on the bed in his motel room and pulled the file from his briefcase. He had to give Russell credit. The report was so complete that Andrew could only marvel at the private investigator's contacts throughout the country. Would it be enough to convince Caitlin's family of her innocence?

The newspaper reports had been damning, but then no one ever claimed that the press was unbiased. While the loss of thirty thousand dollars in a real-estate swindle wouldn't even make the front page in New York City, in Weldon, West Virginia, it had been the headline for two weeks straight.

SIMON REED DISAPPEARS WITH 30K. LOCAL GIRL SOUGHT FOR QUESTIONING DID SHE OR DIDN'T SHE?

D.A SAYS EVIDENCE DOESN'T SUPPORT INDICTMENT OF MS. ADAMS

That didn't stop the people of Weldon from speculating on the guilt of Caitlin Adams. The consensus seemed to be that she was in South America living off her fortune with Simon Reed. Thirty thousand dollars, a fortune? Were they for real? Obviously so, for Caitlin had never set foot in her hometown again.

When he had first read the report, he understood why Caitlin had been reluctant to open up to him. The parallels to his family's past might seem striking. However, while Garret had knowingly gambled with money that wasn't his own, Caitlin had been nothing more than an unwitting pawn.

Simon Reed, alias Simon Raymond, was currently serving seven to ten years in the Ossining Correctional Facility for embezzlement and fraud. Several other charges had to be dropped because the statute of limitations had run out.

Would the fact that Simon Reed had been indicted in seven other states both before and after the incident in Weldon be enough to convince Caitlin's father that Reed had acted alone? Andrew hoped so. Until she could make peace with her family, she would never be at peace with herself. Tyler only made her painfully aware of what she was missing.

He put the file back in the briefcase and took out a map. This morning, when he had come upon Caitlin packing up the wedding dress, she had unknowingly supplied the last piece of information he needed: the exact address of her father's house. He had offered to drop it at the post office and was out the door before Caitlin could protest.

Anger coursed through him when he saw Maggie's return address in the corner. Countless hours of love and hard work had gone into that dress, and Caitlin couldn't even take credit for it. At three o'clock, he decided to leave for the house. He drove through the small towns in the foothills of the Allegheny Mountains, unable to enjoy the scenery. Patches of green flashed by at sixty miles an hour, but his mind remained focused on his meeting with William Adams.

Fifteen minutes later, he pulled up in front of the house. He was unable to believe that the tiny wooden structure had been home to seven people at one time. No wonder they thought thirty thousand dollars was a fortune. He took his briefcase and the box and walked to the front door. The porch step creaked and he actually jumped. Andrew Sinclair, who had never been scared of a single thing in his life, was acting as if he were about to enter the Bates Motel. He wiped a sweaty palm against his suit jacket and took a deep breath before knocking on the door.

A woman in her late fifties—Caitlin's mother, he supposed—answered the door. Grey streaks spattered her dark hair, but her eyes were the same clear green as Caitlin's.

"May I help you?" she said distrustfully.

"My name is Andrew Sinclair. I'm Maggie's brother-in-law. "

The woman stared blankly, then smiled with recognition. "You mean Margaret. I'm sorry. We weren't expecting you. Margaret never mentioned . . ."

"She didn't know I was coming."

She opened the door wider and gestured for him to enter. He was ushered into a small living room. The furnishings had seen better days, but the house was immaculate.

"I'm sorry if this is an inconvenient time, Mrs. Adams."

"Not at all. Have a seat." She pointed to a chair. "And call me Mary, please."

Andrew sat down, but rose immediately when a young woman entered the room. He shook his head in surprise. These Adams sisters certainly did look alike.

"This is my daughter Sissy," Mary said. "Mr. Sinclair is Margaret's brother-in-law."

"Hello, Mr. Sinclair."

"Andrew," he corrected. He handed her the box from the floor. "I believe this is for you."

Sissy shyly took the box, then abandoned her calm as she tore at the brown paper. "It's my dress, isn't it?"

"I believe so."

Mother and daughter sat together and picked through the paper. The lid discarded, Sissy lifted the top half of the dress for inspection. "It's gorgeous."

"Yes," Mary agreed. "You'll have to write your sister a thank-you note."

"I knew Maggie would do it I just knew it!" Sissy gushed.

Andrew bit back an acid retort. Maggie was right when she said her sister was tactless and selfish. "Yes, Caitlin did

138

quite a job on the dress."

Dead silence. They both stared at him in numbed shock.

"You know Caitlin?" Sissy finally asked.

"Yes."

Mary sighed. "Well, of course he must. You probably met at your brother's wedding."

Close enough, he thought. Just the mention of Caitlin made the family nervous. Sissy's gaze darted back and forth between her mother and Andrew. The long silence dragged.

"Sissy, make some coffee for our guest."

Good! A stall tactic. He needed to remain in the house until William Adams returned. "That sounds great."

"Have you seen Margaret's daughter? She hasn't sent a picture yet," Mary said.

"Allison's a little beauty, like her mother." Not as perfect as Tyler, he thought, though not without paternal prejudice.

"She talks about her new house all the time. Says it's right there on the Long Island Sound."

"Yes. The house is wonderful." Andrew wasn't sure how much small talk he could take. Why didn't she ask about the daughter she hadn't seen in ten years? Didn't she have the slightest interest in Caitlin?

By the time the coffee was served, two men came walking through the front door. Caitlin's father and brother, he surmised by their ages. He stood again to greet them.

"This is Andrew Sinclair. His brother is married to Margaret," Mary babbled quickly. Apparently the entire family shared a distrust of strangers.

"My husband William and our son, Sean."

Andrew offered his hand. "A pleasure."

William smiled. "Margaret has mentioned you. You own the company her husband works for."

"Erik is a junior partner, actually."

William removed his jacket and hung it on a peg on the wall. "Please sit."

Andrew was forced to endure ten more minutes of

small talk before he found an opening to get to his point.

Mary's eyes widened hopefully. "Do you have a picture of Allison?"

He had come armed with photographs, including one they might not want to see. He removed the snapshots from his wallet and handed the top one to William.

"That's Maggie with the baby, taken on the steps of her house."

They passed around the picture, clearly impressed by how well their daughter had done.

"And the other?" Sissy asked.

Andrew handed it to William. "That's Caitlin with her son, Tyler."

Dead silence again. William's face remained blank, but he swallowed hard. "I didn't know she was married," he muttered.

Andrew was tired of dancing around the subject. "She's not. Look, Mr. Adams, would it be possible to have a word alone with you?"

Mary stood up. "Come on Sissy, Sean. Let them talk."

Andrew was finally alone with William. The man still hadn't taken his eyes from the picture.

"Mr. Adams, I don't know any other way to do this, so let me come right to the point. I know what happened ten years ago."

William looked up, visibly shaken. "She told you?"

"No. She has no idea I know. What I can't understand is how you could think she was involved. She's your daughter. Don't you know her at all?"

"Mr. Sinclair, you don't know what you're talking about," William grumbled indignantly.

Andrew reached inside his briefcase and pulled out the file, handing it to William. "I know she wasn't involved, and I think I can prove it."

William's eyes darkened. He waved an angry hand and refused the folder. "You don't need to prove my daughter's innocence to me. I've always known it."

"Then, why—"

"You know nothing about life here. There are people

who have hated each other for generations and they can't remember why. It doesn't matter that Caitlin was never charged. Some families lost their life's savings, and that is something they will never forget."

"But it had nothing to do with Caitlin."

"They don't care. They had to blame someone rather than admit a stranger had made fools of them by exposing their greed. If she came back here, I don't think I could protect her. She'd just disappear up in that mountain someday, and the whole town would swear she went back to New York."

Andrew felt an eerie chill run though him. What kind of people were they? "Simon Reed is serving time in jail for a similar crime."

"We're not so backward here that we don't get the news. When he was caught, they hired some fancy lawyer from Wheeling to try to get the money back, but after eight years, there was no way."

"Then this whole thing is about money?" Andrew muttered incredulously.

"Does that shock you? Money does strange things to people. It makes them greedy and violent. In the big cities, they kill a man in the street for ten dollars."

Andrew lowered his head. Money did do strange things to people. He need only look at his own family for proof. It had killed his brother, turned his mother into a vicious shrew and his sister into a troubled young woman heading toward alcoholism.

He gazed at the broken man before him. "If you did this to protect your daughter, why did you never tell her? Why did you let her punish herself for ten years?"

William frowned. "How well do you know my daughter?"

"I think I know her pretty well."

"Then you would know that if I told her the truth, nothing would stop her from coming home to visit her family, regardless of the consequences. Caitlin has always been headstrong. A few years back when my wife was ill, half the town expected Caitlin to come home to see her mama. They had people lookin' for her. Is that what I should subject her to?" William's voice cracked and he turned away.

Andrew gave him a few seconds to compose himself before continuing. "So what you're saying is that it will never be safe for her to return?"

"Not unless those people get their money back. That's the only way they'd acknowledge her innocence. I have four other children. I couldn't pay it back in two lifetimes. And Caitlin wouldn't if she could. It would be the same as admitting guilt."

"If the money were reimbursed, that would be the end of it?"

William regarded him with a mix of skepticism and hope. "You'd pay that money back for Caitlin?"

Andrew shook his head. "No. Not for Caitlin. That would be the same as saying I thought she was guilty."

"Then why?"

"For my son. I think he has the right and the need to know his grandparents, and I find it a small price to pay."

"Your son? Oh, you mean . . ." William glanced at the picture in his hand.

"Yes. Tyler is my son, too." Andrew expected an angry reaction. In William's shoes, he'd be furious. But with all that had passed, William was quietly accepting. It didn't need to be said that after ten years of silence he had no right to judge his daughter's life.

"The money will be paid back, but I don't ever want Caitlin to know where it came from. Or anyone else. I'll have that lawyer in Wheeling send cheques as restitution in the Simon Reed case. No one needs to know we had this conversation. In fact, I was never here."

William blinked and exhaled deeply. Apparently Caitlin's father missed her as much as she missed him. "Caitlin is very lucky to have someone like you."

Andrew broke out in a wry grin. "I doubt she would agree with you, sir. As you said, she can be headstrong and stubborn."

"Oh, yes. When she gets something in her mind, she's

like a mule with a burr in his saddle." Andrew and William shared a laugh over that one. That was Caitlin to a T.

* * * *

Caitlin had insisted on cooking dinner to give Maggie a break. She flipped through a cookbook until she found just what she was looking for. After assembling all the ingredients, she left the pot to simmer on the stove and stepped out onto the deck to enjoy the late afternoon sun.

The two days that Andrew had been gone seemed like an eternity. Perhaps if he had left under better circumstances, she wouldn't have had him in her thoughts all the time. Who was she kidding? Under any circumstances, he was in her thoughts.

She leaned against the rail and turned her face upward. The steady rumble of the ocean lulled her into a state of calm. Eyes closed, she surrendered herself to the smell and feel of the sea air.

An image of Andrew flashed through her mind. His familiar scent lingered as if he were standing right next to her. She ran her tongue across her bottom lip.

"Hungry?" Andrew asked.

She gasped and opened her eyes wide. How had he approached without a sound? Her heart raced, first from fright, then with excitement at the sight of him. Dressed in khaki pants and a short-sleeved safari shirt, he was a vision that far surpassed her imagination.

"What are you doing here?"

"Not even a kiss for the father of your child?"

She let out an exaggerated sigh. "I suppose I could manage that." She wrapped her arms around his neck.

His lips were warm and inviting—then he pulled back. "Whoa, what were you eating? Tabasco sauce?"

Caitlin giggled and slipped out of his arms.

"Sorry. I'm cooking something spicy. I guess that means you don't want a kiss after all."

"Maybe later, when you cool off."

"When I cool off, I won't want to kiss you."

143

"I'll make you want to," he said with that unshakable arrogance of his.

That he was right was beside the point. "Tyler missed you."

Andrew arched an eyebrow. "Did he tell you that?"

"Of course."

He rested his hands on her waist and settled her firmly between his legs as he leaned against the railing. His erection pressed against her stomach, shot a ripple of excitement through her. "And did his mother miss me?"

It took every ounce of willpower she possessed to keep from showing him just how much she missed him, right there on the deck. "She didn't say."

"No, I don't imagine she would. As a matter of fact, I bet she would rather—now what was that quaint expression—oh, yes; she would rather pick the fleas off a mad dog than admit she missed me."

"How did your meeting go?" she asked to change the subject.

For a split second, an odd tension washed over his features, then disappeared behind his seductive grin. "Better than I'd hoped for."

"So Tyler won't have to go visit you in debtors' prison or anything like that?"

"No. Ty is going to have a wonderful life."

"Been staying up late to watch those old movies again?"

For an answer he kissed her again, hard. He urged her backward until they fell together into a lounge chair. Caitlin struggled against him, twisting to free herself from the awkward position before Maggie or Erik joined them.

"Stop fighting me," Andrew muttered in her ear. She knew he was referring to more than their playful encounter. But fighting him was the only way she would emerge from her current situation with her sanity. How could she have been so stupid as to fall in love with him all over again?

"That's better." He apparently took her silence as surrender. She didn't correct him. "Where is everybody?"

"Maggie took the kids for a ride in the car to put them

144

to sleep. They were cranky little monsters. Erik's on the phone with your mother."

"He'll be tied up for hours."

As if on cue, Erik joined them, slumping into a chair with a grunt. "That was the most bizarre conversation I've ever had with Mother."

"What's wrong? Is her credit card over limit again?" Andrew sniped.

"No. She was rattling on about Leslie. Evidently Leslie called the house in a very high-strung state. Sally got the call, and you know how she takes down messages."

Andrew's calm deserted him and he went rigid. "I don't care about Leslie's problems."

"This is scary, Drew. She said something about living at Zenith, the most exhausting day of her life, and a Frenchman who treated her horribly and was going to give her proof. Is she in trouble?"

Andrew groaned. "How would I know? She's probably drunk again."

"What about you, Caitlin?" Erik shot a pointed gaze in her direction. "Can you shed any light on this riddle?"

"Me?" she squeaked out. "How would I know?"

"The message was for you, not mother."

Andrew's fingers tightened around her forearm. "Did she say something to you again?"

"No . . . well, yes . . . not exactly." Caitlin wrinkled her nose at Erik. "She came by the house yesterday after you left. She apologized and asked if the offer of work was still open."

"Leslie work for a living?" Andrew and Erik exclaimed in unison.

She folded her arms across her chest and leveled them both an accusing stare. "It's that very attitude that made her what she is."

"What's that supposed to mean?" Andrew asked.

"Her own brothers thought her so worthless that they wouldn't give her a job. She was merely living up to your expectations of her."

Andrew and Erik exchanged guilty glances.

145

"All right. Then what did the message mean? Is she in trouble?" Andrew asked.

"Probably not. Zenith is probably Zena, one of the models. The Frenchman is actually an American photographer named Anton. He treats the women horribly and they love him. The proofs are still photographs she can use to build a portfolio for a career outside the design centre."

"And what do you know about this Zena she's living with?"

So he did care about his baby sister after all. She snuggled against him in the redwood lounger and smiled. "She's great. I used to live with her myself when I first arrived in New York."

"Why did you help her after what she did?"

"Because she's your sister. More than that, she needed help."

Andrew felt the choked pain in her words. He thought about a beautiful white dress and another sister who didn't deserve Caitlin's help. Family meant everything to her. He could see why Caitlin's father had felt the need to cut off all ties with his daughter. There was nothing Caitlin wouldn't do for her family, even at the expense of her own heart.

"I was thinking . . ." he said.

"Oh, no. That means trouble," she said.

Erik laughed.

Andrew waved a hand at his brother. "Do you mind?" Erik disappeared.

Caitlin twisted against him, slipping her fingers between the buttons of his shirt. "That was rude. This is his house, after all."

"I'll apologize later. Right now, I want to talk to you. What do you think about going away somewhere? You, me, and Tyler. A vacation of sorts."

"When?"

"The first weekend in August sounds good."

The corners of her mouth curved down. "Does it have anything to do with the fact that Maggie and Erik will be attending my sister's wedding that weekend?"

"I hadn't realized," he lied smoothly.

"It's not necessary. I'm all right about it."

"Fine." He shrugged. "Tyler and I will go away. You can stay with Mother."

She clutched his arm desperately. "I take it back. I'd love to go with you."

"You're always disagreeing before you hear what I have to say. If you want me to take you now, I'll need some incentive. What did you make me for dinner?"

A wicked smile spread across her face. "Texas chili. I wanted to see if it's really as hot as you claim."

His body shivered in anticipation. From the way she wriggled against him, he would guess that dinner and dessert would be two spicy numbers. "I'll make the reservations this week."

Chapter Fourteen

After their return from Maggie and Erik's, the atmosphere in the house improved dramatically. Although Joyce would never be considered a warm person, she had begun to tolerate Caitlin's presence; whether from loneliness or fear of her son, Caitlin couldn't tell. By the end of the two-week period she had promised Andrew, she had no grounds to insist on leaving. And in truth, she didn't want to.

July gave way to August. Several times Caitlin asked Andrew where he planned to take her and Tyler. He wouldn't give her so much as a hint. She tried sexual blackmail, but they had so little time alone that she ended up frustrating herself more than him. Without Leslie around, Joyce stayed home most nights, inhibiting any romantic notions Caitlin might have had. Joyce might not know it, but she was getting her revenge.

"Are you all packed?" Andrew asked over breakfast.

Caitlin let out an exasperated sigh. "Since the plane leaves in two hours, I'd better be. Now will you tell me where we're going?"

Andrew took a sip of his coffee and ignored her question. She drummed her fingers against the table to get his attention.

"I'm not telling you," he said simply.

She batted her eyelashes and gave her best imitation of a seductive pout. "Have I ever asked you for anything?"

He choked down his coffee with a hearty chuckle. "Forget it."

"A hint?"

"Somewhere Tyler will enjoy. He'll be showered with attention."

"Disney World?" She smiled. "That's right, isn't it?

He's a little young for that yet."

Andrew shrugged, but she was sure she was right. Where else would he think to take a child?

During the ride to the airport, she whistled the Mickey Mouse Club theme to Tyler. Andrew made her wait in the limo while he checked the bags, but since she already knew where she was going, she let him have his fun. She glanced at the name of the airline and grinned. They were the official carrier for Disney World, if their advertisements were to be believed.

"I'll take Tyler," he said, as she stepped out of the car.

She handed him the baby. "Whatever you say."

They went to the coffee shop and sat down. He wouldn't tell her how long until boarding in case she checked the flight schedule. She folded her hands in her lap and twiddled her thumbs while she stared at a very amused Andrew.

She felt a tap on her shoulder and turned. "Hiya."

Caitlin's eyes widened. "Maggie? What are you doing here?"

"Going to Sissy's wedding, same as you."

"No. We're going to Disney World, right Andrew?" When she didn't get an answer, she straightened to face him. "Andrew?"

"I never said that."

For a few dazed seconds, the words didn't register in her mind. Confusion was rapidly replaced by panic. The air seemed to be sucked from the room and she couldn't breathe. She gasped. "No. I'm not going."

She sprang to her feet and reached for Tyler. Andrew snuggled the baby against his chest.

"You're going, Caitlin." He handed her a boarding pass.

"I don't think you understand, Andrew. I can't go," she said.

Maggie put a hand on her shoulder. "It's okay. You're invited."

"No one called me."

"They didn't know your number, and I was afraid you

149

might not go if I told you, so I sort of asked Andrew to help me."

Caitlin gaped at her sister. She couldn't believe Maggie, of all people, would do this to her. Had a few important details slipped her mind? Like what had happened ten years ago, or that Andrew had tried to sue her for custody less than two months ago?

She yanked Maggie by the arm out of the coffee shop and into the corridor. "Are you crazy? I can't go there with Andrew."

"Sissy said you could bring a date."

"Maggie, you don't understand. Andrew doesn't know what happened. Does he?" Her stomach lurched at the horrible possibility. "Did you tell him?"

"No!" Maggie said. "No one will mention it."

"How can you be sure?"

"Daddy promised."

Great! Maggie had discussed Caitlin's personal life with her father. "Does Daddy know about Tyler, too?"

"That's up to you to tell them."

"Then I definitely can't go there with Tyler and Andrew. What will they think?"

"Only what you tell them. Please, Caitlin. Mom is so excited. She called every day to make sure you were coming."

"I can't."

Erik stepped into the hall with Allison strapped to his back. "Ladies. The plane is boarding."

Caitlin gestured helplessly. "Tell Andrew to come back here."

Erik gave her a sympathetic smile. "He's already on the plane."

"Well, tell him to get off."

"You go tell him. Come on, Maggie. Let your sister make her own decision."

What kind of decision did she have? Her son was on the plane. She couldn't leave him. Her only hope was to get away in the airport in Wheeling and take the next flight back.

150

Andrew was feeling rather pleased with the way things were turning out. Maggie may have thought she planned this little scheme, but only because he and Erik had set it up that way. Given a choice, he was sure Caitlin would have refused to go home with him. He wanted to be there for her if she needed him, only she would never admit that she needed him.

She stormed onto the plane in a fit of fury. Tyler's car seat was buckled into the window seat and Andrew had the aisle, leaving her the middle. As she passed in front of him, she dug her spiked heel into his foot.

He didn't acknowledge the excruciating pain. "I hope you didn't want the window seat. I had them give it to Tyler."

"I can see that, Andrew. I'm not blind as well as stupid." She wasn't taking this as well as he had imagined.

"Nothing is as bad as you think."

She grunted and looked away.

He cupped her face in his fingers and turned her head back. "I'm talking to you. They made the first move. It's up to you now. If you can't do it for them, do it for Tyler."

"That's not the problem."

"If I'm the problem, I won't go to the house. I'll stay at the hotel. I know you're afraid of something and there's more to the story than you told me, but I don't care what happened. I promise you, I will never use it to take Tyler from you."

She blinked. "How did you know?"

"I told you once that no judge would have given me custody of Tyler. You're still afraid of me. There has to be a reason."

Caitlin was afraid of many things; Andrew was now the least of them. Why had her father suddenly allowed her to come home? Why not ten years ago, when she begged to return? Or last year when Maggie had come in search of her? Taking the next flight back to New York wouldn't give her those answers, and after all this time, she needed answers. "All right, I'll go."

"Do you want me to stay at the hotel?"

"No way. When my father goes off the deep end about Tyler, I want him aiming the buckshot for your south end, not mine."

Andrew laughed. "That Adams spite rears its ugly head."

"Serves you right. I wanted to go to Disney World."

He laced his fingers through hers. "Enjoy the flight."

Caitlin expelled a puff of air. Like she had any chance of enjoying the flight with all she had to worry about.

* * * *

"I'm not talking to you," Caitlin informed Maggie in the hotel lobby.

"Why?"

She shivered from the air conditioning and a bad case of nerves. "You should have warned me so I would be more prepared."

Maggie arched an eyebrow. "You would have prepared by taking a flight to Singapore. And what's the difference if Andrew does hear what happened? It's over, or Daddy never would have invited you to the wedding."

"Yeah. It is kind of strange. It makes me wonder . . ."

What had happened to bring about this unexpected invitation? Her parents had known where to find her for months. Was Sissy's marriage to Quinton Fletcher behind the change of attitude?

"We're on the third floor," Andrew broke into her thoughts. "The elevators are around the corner.

"What time are you leaving for the house?" she asked her sister.

"About four. I want to be there for dinner. What about you?"

"Monday at five."

"That's when we go back," Andrew said.

"I can't put anything past you," Caitlin joked. "I guess we'll leave about the same time. I need to relax for a few hours."

Relax? More like work herself into such a state of anxiety they would have to rush her to the hospital. She stroked her finger along Tyler's cheek as he rested in his father's arms. For ten years she had dreamed about this day. Now that it had arrived, she wasn't ready.

* * * *

Caitlin stared at the small house as if she were seeing a ghost. Her body trembled. Andrew had to take Tyler from her for fear she might drop him. He hadn't expected her to be quite this apprehensive. She changed her clothes four times before he had finally gotten her out the door.

Thankfully, her nervous state had stopped her from noticing that he didn't need directions to find her father's house. Another slip and she would easily figure out that he had been here before.

"Are you going to stand here and admire the architecture?" he asked.

"Just a minute," she whispered.

He draped his arm across her shoulder. "They know you're here. They must have heard the car."

She pushed an unsteady hand through her hair. "I can't."

"Don't tell me that the girl who beat up all the boys in Mrs. Ketchum's fifth-grade class is afraid to walk into her own house."

At the sound of the familiar voice, Caitlin spun around. "Sean." Her choked voice was barely audible.

The tall figure stepped forward, blocking the setting sun. Thick dark hair fell across his forehead. His mouth lifted in a crooked grin. "Have I changed so much?"

She shook her head.

"Lord, Caitlin, we never used to be able to shut you up," Sean teased.

"People change," she said sorrowfully.

Sean took another step forward and pulled her into a bear hug. "You know, they're just as scared as you are.

153

Maybe even more."

"I doubt that." She took a deep breath and pulled away.

Tyler let out a gurgle to make his presence known. She took him from Andrew. "Where are my manners? Sean, this is Andrew and our son, Tyler."

Sean shook hands with Andrew, then stretched his arms out for the baby. "Could I?"

She nodded and handed Sean the child in a state of obvious bewilderment. Andrew knew she had expected her family to be shocked or outraged, not accepting, and he was thrilled for her. But he knew this could backfire on him. Once she made peace with her family, any threat she felt from him would be gone. If she chose to move back to her apartment or even back home with her parents, he couldn't stop her.

The front door opened and Sissy stepped onto the porch with her hands on her hips. "Quit your lollygagging, Caitlin. It's Friday, your night to set the table. If you think hiding outside with Sean until it's too late is still gonna work, you're wrong."

She smiled even while tears streamed down her cheeks. "I'll pay you a quarter to do it for me. A dollar if you wash the dishes, too."

"She doesn't wash dishes," Sean muttered dryly. "She might break a nail before the wedding."

Caitlin spun back toward her brother and winked. "Is she really marrying Quinton? Daddy must be over the moon."

Sean handed Tyler back to her and walked her toward the house. "He's more excited about seeing you. Why don't you go put him out of his misery? You may not believe this, but it broke his heart to do what he did to you."

"What's he going to say about Tyler?"

"He'll probably say how beautiful the baby is. There isn't a one of us who's earned the right to pass judgment on you, except possibly your shadow."

The reference to Maggie eased her mind. Turning to Andrew, she raised a smile. "Are you coming?"

"You go say hello first. I want to stay out here with

Sean and hear how you beat up the entire fifth grade."

She shrugged. "Someone had to defend Sean."

"Well, I would have preferred it wasn't my sister," Sean grumbled bashfully and gave her a little push toward the door.

"Come on, Ty. After Daddy's house, this should be a piece of cake."

Tyler reached for the barrette in her hair. She shifted him to her hip and climbed the stairs. The third step still creaked. With one last look at Andrew, she walked through the door.

Four anxious faces stared up at her. Despite the years, her parents seemed to have changed little.

Maggie sent her a reassuring smile from across the room. "I don't think introductions are necessary."

"They might be." Caitlin glanced at her youngest sister, who had been barely three when she left. "You can't be Kelly."

"Yes, I am."

"I guess you don't remember me."

"You're my sister Caitlin. Mama told me."

Just a name that had to be told to her. That hurt. "Well, this is Tyler. He needs an aunt to look after him. Do you think you could do that for me?"

Kelly looked over the new arrival as Caitlin placed him in her lap. "He doesn't look Oriental."

A nervous laugh escaped. Apparently Maggie had said something. "He was born in Singapore, but he was made from American parts."

She raised her head and gazed around the room. Why didn't anyone say anything? They stared at her, motionless, as if she were an apparition. Her courage was rapidly fading. "Would somebody say something, please?"

After an uncomfortable pause, her father stood up. She remembered him being so much bigger. Was it time or merely her memory that had changed him? "What do you say to someone you've done the unforgivable to? What are the right words?" William's voice broke with emotion.

"You say hello, Daddy. If it were unforgivable, I

155

wouldn't be here."

Her father pulled her into his arms. His body shook and he held her so tight she could barely breathe. "I'm so glad you came. I wasn't sure you would."

"I would have come anytime you called me. Why did you wait so long?"

"There are a lot of things I have to explain, but not right now. You're mama's been driving everyone crazy around here. If you don't give her a hug, I think she'll explode."

"If you squeeze me any harder, I might explode," she said.

"Turn her loose, Will, she's turning blue," Mary reprimanded her husband. But the second he let go of Caitlin, she was grabbed by her mother. By the time she had gone around the room, she felt battered and bruised . . . and strangely at peace.

While her parents fussed over Tyler and Allison, Caitlin leaned against the wall next to Maggie. She smoothed her dress over her hips and sighed. "I'm whipped."

"I guess you're not mad at me anymore."

"No." She glanced toward her laughing son. "They seem to have taken the news about Tyler well. Thanks for filling them in."

"I didn't ..."

Maggie's words were cut off by Sissy's whining voice. "Quit hogging Caitlin's time. You see her all the time. I want to talk to her, too."

Maggie never finished what she had started to say. Instead, she leaned in closer and whispered in Caitlin's ear. "Who is she kidding? She wants the dress off your back and any others you might be willing to part with."

Caitlin laughed. Nothing had changed. "Where are Andrew and Erik?"

"Outside with Sean. He's sick to death of hearing about Quinton. But I guess we can't get out of it."

Sissy pulled Caitlin down on the couch next to her. "You're not upset that I'm marrying Quinton, are you?"

"No," Caitlin assured her while trying to keep a straight face. "How did the dress fit?"

"Perfect. Daddy nearly blew a gasket when he found out you made it, but I told him you didn't care.

"You're wrong, Sissy. It's precisely because I care that I made the dress. I wish you had asked me yourself." She hadn't intended to carp, but she needed answers for her own satisfaction.

"We made mistakes," her mother said softly. "We can't change that."

Caitlin's eyes spilled over with tears. She brushed them away with a shaky hand. For ten years, she had kept a tight rein on her emotions, but today she was losing the battle with herself.

"I know you can't change it, Mama, but why didn't you believe in me? Every birthday, every Christmas, I made myself sick with sorrow, and I want to know why."

"Caitlin," her father called through the screen door. "I think it's time we had a talk."

Of course, she thought. Everything in the house was done on her father's orders. He had decided that she must never return and his word had ended that banishment. Now she would finally know why so she could get on with the rest of her life.

Chapter Fifteen

The sky was aflame in deep reds and oranges as the sun dipped below the mountain. Caitlin and William walked in silence. He seemed to have a thousand things to say, but not a single word came out of his mouth.

Suddenly, he stopped. He leaned against a tree and cleared his throat "I always knew you were innocent. I couldn't tell you that because I knew you'd come back if I did."

"Wasn't that the idea, Daddy?"

He slumped his shoulders and stared at the ground as he spoke. "When Simon Reed left here, those people wanted blood. They didn't care whose. If you had set foot in Weldon, your life wouldn't have been worth anything. I couldn't do that to you. I'd rather have you hate me and be alive."

"You only made it worse by disowning me. They became more convinced of my guilt." That had hurt more than anything. She had been so close to her father.

"I had four other children. Since I didn't have the money or the ability to fight what was being said, I did the only thing I could to protect you all."

His voice cracked and he turned away. The tower of strength she always remembered was crumbling. The choice must have been a torment for him.

"Why didn't you tell me this before?"

"You're too damned stubborn for your own good. You would have come back to visit. It was safer to let you think you weren't welcome."

On that count, her father was probably right. She still had a lot of unanswered questions. "Why is it safe now?"

"Simon Reed was caught and sent to prison."

"When?"

"Two years ago."

"Two years?" she cried out. "Why didn't you tell me then?"

Lines of sorrow etched his weathered features. "They only just got the money back. A lot of people were taking him to court. Until the money was returned, you weren't fully cleared."

"And when was that?"

William paused nervously. He ran a hand along his square jaw. "Two weeks ago the money was transferred to the bank in town. People started coming around here and telling me how they knew you weren't involved all along. Damned hypocrites, all of them."

A decade of her life lost because of money. Money that people were too greedy to hold on to. How pathetic when people could put a dollar amount on a human life. At thirty thousand dollars, she wasn't cheap.

"You have no idea how much it hurt to do that to you. I'm more sorry than I can tell you, Caitlin, but if I had to do it all over again, I'd do the same thing. And before you judge me, ask yourself, what would you do to protect your child?"

"Whatever it took," she whispered in agreement. She wiped a hand across her tear-stained cheeks. "Maybe I understand more than I used to."

"But can you forgive me?"

She smiled. "There was never any question of that."

William hugged his daughter. "Should we go back to the house before they send a search party?"

"Oh, Daddy, we could never get lost in these mountains."

"I don't think your city man knows that."

She hooked her arm through her father's. "Don't let the clothes fool you. Underneath. .

"Now don't go telling your dad that you've seen what's underneath that man's clothes. I'd be forced to take out my shotgun to defend your honour."

For the first time since her return, she genuinely laughed. How did her father imagine Tyler was conceived?

But it was an amusing thought. She could just imagine Andrew's face if he were offered a shotgun wedding. He'd most likely opt for quick death.

When she returned to the house, she found the object of her affections making himself quite at home in the living room, with her mother and Sissy fawning over him. He did know how to get the ladies to worship at his feet. While she had feared that Andrew might feel uncomfortable in the modest surroundings, he seemed more content than she had seen him in a long time. It must be the mountain air, she decided.

Sean sat in the dining room amusing Tyler.

"Do you want me to take over?" Caitlin asked.

"Nah. I got him," Sean said. He put a finger under Ty's chin. "This baby is the spitting image of his daddy, but he sure doesn't look like you. Are you sure you're the mother?"

Caitlin gazed toward Andrew. "Yeah, the poor kid is destined to go through life looking like his daddy. What a hardship! He'll probably grow up to be every bit as arrogant, too."

"Shame on you, Caitlin," Sissy admonished.

Andrew chuckled. "Don't listen to her. I don't."

The second Sissy's attention was diverted, Caitlin stuck the tip of her tongue out and ran it seductively across her lips. Andrew's body temperature rose twenty degrees. He fanned a hand in front of his face to let her know the message had been received.

Caitlin had relaxed visibly in the last half-hour, Andrew noted with a smug sense of satisfaction. With the issues of her past finally resolved, he might be able to discuss their future.

"What time is dinner, Mom?"

"About six, when Quinton gets here. You go have a seat next to Andrew while I get some coffee," Mary said. The older woman gestured Sissy out of the room. She had even conveniently sent the others out of the house.

Caitlin smiled at her mother's blatant matchmaking efforts. "My mother must really like you," she said, as she fell into the seat beside him. "I've never known her to call any man by his given name the first day she meets him."

His smile never faded, but the knot in his stomach tightened. Luckily, Caitlin wasn't looking for signs of his involvement, because she'd had enough of them. He slid his arm across her shoulder and edged her closer. "What can I say? I have the kind of face people trust."

"I will refrain from the obvious retort, because today is a special day."

"Is it? You're not still angry that I forced you on the plane?"

She rested her head on his shoulder. "I'm not sure. I had my heart set on Disney World. Let's see if you can make it up to me before Monday."

A grin spread across his face. "Don't you think I'm up to the challenge?"

"Don't make me talk dirty in my father's house."

"All right. You just keep those racy thoughts to yourself. I know what you want."

"I know. That's the problem."

Before he could decide how to take her response, Mary arrived with a tray of steaming coffee.

Caitlin sent her mother a grateful smile and reached for a cup. "Boy, do I need this."

"No dear, that's Andrew's. It has no sugar," Mary said, then discretely returned to the kitchen.

Caitlin wrinkled her nose in distaste and handed him the cup, then reached for the other.

"Now, about tomorrow. I suggest you take your brother and run, because I won't be held responsible for the trouble my father and brother might get you into."

"I'll keep that in mind. What about tonight? Do you want to stay here with your family?"

"Oh, sure, Andrew. I'd much rather sleep in a cramped room with two sisters than with you," she joked. "Is that your preference, too?"

He exhaled a groan. "No. I want you in my bed. But what about Tyler?"

"We have a two-room suite. I have an intercom. By the

time we leave here, he'll be so exhausted it will take an atom bomb to wake him before morning."

"I see you've worked out every detail."

"Not everyone. I prefer spontaneity. I wouldn't want to become too predictable."

Predictable? So many facets of Caitlin were still a mystery. She guarded her emotions closely and he wasn't sure what she felt for him—except when they made love. Then she was easy to read. She gave everything and expected the same from him.

He had his doubts, though, if she would be up for much tonight. She curled into his body and closed her eyes; her warm breathing along his neck became deep and rhythmic. All of Mary's matchmaking efforts had been for nothing.

* * * *

Hushed voices invaded Caitlin's restless sleep. The entire family must have returned to the house. She opened her heavy eyelids and looked up at Andrew, who was talking to someone above them. She turned her head to follow his gaze. Maggie stood with Tyler in her arms.

"Welcome back," Andrew whispered.

"How long have I been out?" she mumbled.

"A half hour."

A half hour? With company arriving any minute! She struggled to a sitting position and smoothed the fabric of her dress. Too late, she discovered, when she saw Sissy wrapped up in her fiancé's arms.

Tyler began to whimper and she immediately got to her feet. Any excuse to exit the room was welcome. "Thanks for waking me," she grumbled to Maggie as she took Tyler.

"Andrew said you needed to rest for a while."

Oh, he did? Andrew was acting very peculiar. Why would he want her sleeping in his lap when Quinton arrived? Was he jealous of her old boyfriend? That didn't fit her image of Andrew. Maybe she didn't know him as well as she thought. Despite her constant protests, he had done everything in his power to make her life easier.

She knew better than to question fate, but something wasn't right. Her life was coming together too smoothly, as if someone had scripted a happily-ever- after ending onto a soap opera. What had she overlooked?

When Tyler began to cry in earnest, her thoughts were immediately diverted. She took him into her parents' room to feed him and was soon joined by Andrew, who had turned watching his son nurse into a daily ritual. "You'll shock my mother if she finds you in here while I'm doing this."

"What's one more shock today?" He sat behind her on the bed and wrapped his arms around her and Tyler. The warmth of his body blanketed her in comfort. Moments like this could almost make her believe in a future with him.

He nipped playfully at her earlobe.

"Damn it, Andrew, don't get me excited while I'm feeding the baby. He's liable to grow up with all kinds of hang-ups."

"He'll grow up just fine, Caitlin. And in another twenty years, he'll discover a whole new interest in the female breast." He ran a featherlike stroke along her arm, then slipped his hand inside her dress to cup her breast as Tyler suckled.

The jolt to her system was so intense that even Tyler jumped. "Please, Andrew."

"Please stop or please continue?"

"Just hold that thought a couple of hours." She elbowed him in his side. "Why don't you go back out there and talk to the company?"

"Your ex?" he said with a laugh.

"You jealous?"

"Not after meeting him. Did your father really expect you to marry that—"?"

"Careful. He's going to be my brother-in-law. If you can't say something nice . . ."

"Something nice?" He drummed his fingers against her thigh as he tried to find one kind word to say about the

163

pompous bag of wind in the other room. "He has a beautiful sister-in-law."

"How sweet. I'll be sure to tell Maggie you said that."

"You don't take compliments very well."

She nodded. "I know. I don't like them when they have to do with my looks. Unfortunately, that's the only kind I'm likely to get in this town."

Andrew knew exactly what she was thinking. Resentment burned in her eyes. Resentment for a town that had ostracized her for years, had made her doubt herself. And particularly resentment for Quinton Fletcher, who should have stood up for her then, instead of taking all the credit for getting the money back now.

There were a hundred things he wanted to say to her about Quinton Fletcher and the Simon Reed case. But unless she brought up the subject, he had to remain silent.

She tilted her head back and gazed into his eyes. "Can I ask you something?"

"Anything . . . except—"

She laughed. "I wasn't going to ask to move back to my apartment."

"Okay." He nodded for her to continue.

"Why did you want to come here?"

His eyebrows arched in question. "Why do you think?"

Silky strands of hair tickled his neck as she shook her head. "I don't know. To tell you the truth, nothing makes sense anymore. It's like I never left. My parents react to everything I tell them as if they already knew, but Maggie swears she never told them anything."

Guilt gnawed at his insides. He tried to convince himself that omission was not lying, but he wasn't buying it. Maybe he shouldn't have told her family so much about her life, but they had been so desperate for any scrap of information.

"They want to make you feel at home."

"It's more than that. I half expected my father to put a shotgun to your head and demand you make an honest woman out of me."

Andrew choked back a laugh. He'd half expected that

himself when he first told William. Hell, a part of Andrew wished the old man had. It would be easier than getting up the courage to make Caitlin an offer she might refuse. "Thanks for the warning. Your father invited me hunting tomorrow, but now I'm afraid he plans to hunt me."

"I'm serious, Andrew. Why did you come?"

"To meet my son's family." She narrowed her eyes in disbelief. "All right. I wasn't sure how you were going to react and I thought you might need me."

For a long moment she said nothing. Finally, she smiled. "I'm glad you came."

"So am I."

She handed Tyler to Andrew to burp while she straightened her dress. "Let's get this dinner over so that we don't have to spend the entire evening with Quinton."

"Is that the only reason you want to go back to the hotel in a hurry?"

She winked and blew him a kiss. "What other reason could there be?"

* * * *

Caitlin pushed Andrew's hand away for the third time in as many seconds. She tried to squirm off the bed, but his arm kept her firmly anchored next to him. "Cut it out. I have to go to the house to help out my mother."

That was just an excuse. She needed to catch her breath. Andrew's stamina was awesome. They had been up since six o'clock. Tyler had nursed and had gone right back to sleep, but she had been kept in a state of continuous arousal since.

A glance at Andrew's silly grin, and she knew he wasn't buying her excuse.

"No one expects you this early. We don't get much time alone as it is. We have to make the most of it."

At the rate he was going, he'd be set for the next year.

"Don't you ever get tired?" she asked.

"I could never get tired of making love to you." He slid his hand along her stomach and down to her thigh.

Her reaction was rapid and acute. Heat burned in her lower abdomen and she instinctively arched against his open palm. She groaned.

"Couldn't you pretend to be tired? For ten minutes?" She blew a wisp of hair off her forehead and reached for the intercom. "Come on, Ty, wake up."

Andrew chuckled. "Let him sleep. The poor kid's exhausted."

"So's his mama."

"Then I guess I couldn't interest you in a nice hot shower."

She smiled wryly. "Who said that?"

Andrew slid off the bed. Caitlin tried to follow, but her sore limbs protested. Every muscle ached. Her breasts were tender and a moist feeling burned deep inside her. She was more tired than she ever thought possible, and she had never felt more alive.

"Having trouble?" Andrew asked.

"I could use a little help."

He came over to the bed. "What would you like me to do?"

"Put your clothes on?" she suggested hopefully. Just the sight of his naked body made her ache for him again. As he leaned over to lift her, she wrapped her arms around his neck and tugged him down on top of her.

His body pressed to hers, searing her with the pure strength and silky smoothness of hot, hard flesh. He balanced his weight on his elbows and hovered just slightly above her. "I thought you were tired."

"I caught a second wind." Or a fifth wind, by this point. She wriggled beneath him, urging him to join with her.

"Patience, Caitlin."

She arched to him, inhaling sharply as he entered her. Andrew's control contrasted with her own abandon. A control, she quickly discovered that was nothing more than a facade, easily stripped away. He was no more patient than she was. Release came quickly and with violent intensity.

Long after her breathing had returned to normal, she

166

gazed into his eyes. God, how she loved this man. She wanted to tell him, but the words died on her lips as he pressed a kiss against her mouth. Perhaps it was just as well that she didn't tell him. If he didn't share her feelings, she didn't want to know. At least, not yet.

Chapter Sixteen

Caitlin watched from the front porch as the truck disappeared around a winding bend.

"Do you think we should have stopped them?" Maggie asked.

"Not on your life. I only wish I could have convinced Sean to take the camera along. If Andrew's naive enough to think we still hunt and eat possum in the mountains, then he deserves everything he has coming."

"Oh, you're rotten to him."

"Maybe, but I almost envy him today." With a forlorn sigh, she reached for the door handle. "Let's go help Mom set up for the shower."

"I can't wait." Excitement bubbled in Maggie's voice.

"I can." Caitlin wrinkled her nose in distaste. "I'm in no hurry to see those people."

"You should revel in it. Don't you know what they say about living well being the best revenge? Well, rest assured, by the time I'm finished, there won't be a person in the town of Weldon who doesn't know how well you've done."

There was a time when Caitlin would have wanted nothing more. Now just being able to see her family again was enough. "Forget it, Maggie. There's no point."

"Okay. Then you'd better get inside before Sissy picks your suitcase clean. Apparently she wants to impress these people, even if she has to steal your clothes to do it."

Caitlin smiled. When she had left the hotel with her suitcase this morning, Andrew had accused her of trying to run away from him. "Let her have 'em."

She pushed open the screen door. Her mother looked to be in heaven, sitting on the floor of the living room with her two babbling grandchildren. Sissy was sitting on the couch, rooting through the open case.

"Are you sure you don't mind, Caitlin?" Sissy asked, not sounding the least bit concerned. She looked over another dress and added it to the pile of clothes she wanted to keep.

Caitlin glanced at the discard pile, which consisted of exactly two T-shirts. "No, I don't mind. But would you let me keep that teal one until after the bridal shower?"

"Oh, sure. But try not to spill anything on it today," Sissy joked. At least Caitlin hoped she was joking. Sissy took the clothes to her room to hang them up.

Mary shook her head. "I swear, if she didn't look so much like the rest of you, I would sue the hospital for a mix-up. But you have to forgive her. She was mighty embarrassed when her younger sister got married before her."

Maggie shrugged her shoulders. "I can't help it. Erik wanted to get married right away."

"You might even thank Andrew for that," Caitlin quipped.

Maggie threw a pillow at her sister. "Give him a break, Caitlin. How much longer do you intend to punish him before you forgive him?"

"Why would you want to punish him?" Mary asked. "He's such a charming young man."

Caitlin rolled her eyes. Just what she needed. Encouragement from the Andrew Sinclair fan club. She remembered their early morning lovemaking and blushed. If that was punishment, he would be impossible forever.

"Look at her red cheeks, Mama. I think she's in love with him but won't admit it," Maggie taunted. "Come on Jell-O Legs, admit it."

Caitlin grunted. "Never. I have to keep him on his toes. I told him not to stand in front of Daddy today while they're hunting, just in case."

"You didn't," Mary cried out, mortified. "What will he think?"

"He laughed at me. He always laughs at me. He's a stubborn mule and he makes me crazy." And she loved

169

every blessed minute of it.

Mary bowed her head thoughtfully. "Yep, she loves him all right."

"Are we here to work or to discuss my love life?"

Caitlin tried to ignore the knowing grins from her mother and sister and get back to the task of setting up for the shower. The sooner this day was over with, the better.

* * * *

An eerie wind whistled through the trees. Sunset framed the mountain in vibrant shades of purple and red. Caitlin could see the house in the distance as she perched herself up in her favourite tree.

The shower had been a great success. Some of the women had stopped to talk to her, claiming they'd always known she was innocent. Damned hypocrites, all of them, her father had said. He was right. Still, she had enjoyed seeing them swallow a large helping of humble pie.

Her mother and sisters were off on a late afternoon trip to the mall, but Caitlin had declined. She wanted solitude and a chance to figure out the puzzle that had become her life.

The sound of approaching footsteps broke her short-lived peace.

Sean leaned against the tree. "I know you're up there."

She dropped herself to the ground. "Am I so predictable?"

"You were never predictable."

No, she had to agree, she had never been much of a conformist. If she had been, perhaps her life might have turned out differently. For sure, she would have steered clear of Simon Reed. Her life had been lonely, but it must have been worse for her family.

"How come you never married, Sean?"

"With what money? I barely make enough at the warehouse to live at home."

She kicked at a small stone. "Maybe you should try New York. Union workers make good money there."

"I've heard. Andrew and Erik said I could work for them if I wanted."

She couldn't hide her surprise. "Are you thinking about it?"

"Would you be mad if I said yes?"

"What a ridiculous question."

Sorrow marred his handsome features. "I didn't talk to you for ten years. I wasn't sure if you understood why we did it. I know Maggie never did."

Caitlin touched his arm. "I think she does now. You see things differently when you have a child of your own."

"I guess so," he said grudgingly. "Is that why you didn't want Andrew to know about what happened? Did you think you were protecting your child?"

"Maggie has a motor mouth," she said with a laugh.

Sean put his arm across her shoulder and walked her toward the house. "Actually, Andrew was the one who told me. He'd never do anything to hurt you or Tyler."

"Oh, yeah? Did he mention that he tried to sue me for custody?"

"Yep. He also said he was only trying to get your attention."

She laughed. "Well, he got my attention, all right."

Sean tugged on the ponytail hanging down her back. "It's your own fault. You can be downright rigid when you want to be."

"I am extremely flexible." She raised her chin defiantly.

"So is iron, but only after you get it hot enough."

"Andrew does have a knack for getting me hot," she agreed and regretted the words the second they were out of her mouth.

"I'd say that's obvious."

"Sean!" She raised her hand to playfully smack him. He grabbed her wrist in mid swing and twisted her arm behind her back.

"You're in love with the guy. Admit it."

She squirmed and twisted and laughed. "Never." When they were younger, she'd had no trouble beating the tar out

171

of her brother. He was now much bigger and stronger than she was, and her efforts to escape were futile.

"You know it's true. We don't lie to each other."

"I didn't say it wasn't true. I said I'd never admit it."

"Are you afraid?" he taunted.

"I'm afraid that if you don't let me go, I will physically assault you."

"You and what army?" He chuckled and tightened his grip.

After ten years of living in New York, she had learned a thing or two about self-defence. She would have preferred her spiked heels, but her sneaker still landed on his foot with enough force to make Sean loosen his grip. Once free, she darted back to the house and was inside the door before he caught up to her.

She flopped down on the sofa next to her father. With her hands folded in her lap, she looked the picture of innocence. She shot Sean a triumphant grin.

"What was that about?" Andrew asked.

William put his arm around his daughter's shoulder and grinned. "I'd say Caitlin just learned she can't beat up her brother anymore."

Andrew's eyes sparkled with amusement. "You're lucky she doesn't have her heels on."

"Those sneakers are lethal too," Sean said, rubbing his sore foot. "You vicious, mule-headed brat."

Caitlin pursed her lips in a pout. "Are you gonna let him talk to me like that, Daddy?"

"Go ahead. Get Dad on your side. I'll just have a talk with Andrew and tell him what we were discussing when you attacked me," Sean threatened.

"You wouldn't dare," Caitlin warned.

"What's my silence worth to you?"

"Whatever she says, I'll double it if you tell me," Andrew interjected.

"You can't buy off family," Caitlin said.

Sean waved his hand to cut her off. "Wait. I haven't heard his offer yet."

Andrew's laughter was more than she could take. He

172

had made a place for himself with her family and, although she was loathe to admit it, she was jealous.

She got up and went to check on Tyler. He was still sleeping, so she sat down on the bed rather than return to the living room.

She had thought returning home would clear up so many of the questions that had plagued her. If anything, she was only more confused. Why couldn't she leave well enough alone? Hoping to distract her suspicions, she reached for the photo album on her mom's dresser. The pictures of all the birthdays and graduations she had missed left her feeling melancholy.

She turned over the last page and froze. The room felt as cold as death. This very picture of her and Tyler used to be on Andrew's bedside table.

That was it—the missing piece of the puzzle. Her family wasn't surprised about Tyler or anything else about her life because they already knew. How had her mother come to have the picture? There was only one explanation. Fragmented pieces of conversations rang in her ears.

He doesn't look Oriental. How had Kelly known that Tyler was born in Singapore?

That's Andrew's coffee. It has no sugar. How could her mother know how Andrew took his coffee unless . . .

My mother must really like you. I've never known her to call any man by his given name the first time she meets him. Yesterday wasn't the first time Mary had met him.

But when? How? He had never been away, except for his business meeting two weeks ago. Two weeks ago the money was transferred to the bank in town.

Andrew knew all along about her past. What an idiot she was! She had never been cleared in the Simon Reed case. He had bought them off. The pain in her heart was beyond tears. She removed the picture from the album and walked back into the living room, completely numb.

* * * *

The   moment   Andrew   saw   Caitlin's   pale,

173

expressionless face, his stomach knotted. "What's the matter?"

"I guess I was wrong, Andrew. You can buy off family."

"What are you talking about?"

She held the picture out. When he didn't take it, she flung it at him. "You've been here before, haven't you?"

Andrew wasn't sure which was colder, her eyes or her heart. He never should have left the picture. He couldn't lie. She already knew the answer. "Yes."

"You lousy bastard. You paid that money. It was never settled in court."

"Caitlin, we'll have no cussing in this house," her father said.

"What are you going to do? Kick me out for another ten years? Maybe Andrew will just pay you off again."

She folded her arms across her chest and glowered contemptuously at Andrew. "Thirty thousand dollars. When you figure out how much time we've actually had together, that pretty much makes me the most expensive whore in America. I hope you got your money's worth."

She was out the door before anyone could say a word. Her father rose to follow her, but Andrew stopped him.

"No. She didn't mean what she said to you. I'm the one she's angry with. I have to talk to her first."

He walked outside into the cool night air. His proud stance might have been more foolish than he realized. How was he supposed to find her in the pitch dark? This was her home, but he'd be lost in the mountains.

And after he found her, what was he supposed to say? He had only seen that look in her eyes once before, and he swore he would never be the one to put it there again. Hurting Caitlin was the last thing he wanted to do.

Keeping the lights from the house visible at all times, he walked up the mountain. The distance grew, and the light became fainter. The chirping of crickets seemed to mock him. He was about to give up and wait for her to return on her own when he heard leaves crunching under light footsteps.

174

"Caitlin?"

"Go away."

He turned in the direction of her voice and took a few more steps before he saw her. "May I explain first?"

"Explain how you paid off a town for your whore? That's what they'll all think." Her voice cracked as she tried to speak through her tears. She ran her sleeve across her face and sniffed.

Nothing caused him more pain than to hear her cry.

He took another step closer. "No one knew about the money except your father, and now Sean."

"Were you ever going to tell me?"

"No," he admitted.

"How could you do that? How could you think I was guilty in the first place?" The anguish in her voice ripped through him.

"That thought never crossed my mind."

"Then why did you pay back the money?"

"Because it was the only way you would be able to return safely."

A tiny hiccup escaped between her shallow breaths. "What's it to you if I could return or not?"

"You were unhappy." There was a long pause.

She turned and met his gaze. "Do you think I'm happy now?"

He placed his hand along her cheek and smiled weakly. "Not at this particular moment, but I'm the one you're mad at, not your father."

"You're wrong." She pushed his hand away. She wasn't ready to accept comfort from him. "I'm furious with both of you. I am so humiliated. What gave you the right to interfere?"

"You did."

"When?"

"When you had Tyler. Didn't you tell me how important grandparents are? What you and Tyler have with my mother is about as warm as it gets. I can't do anything about that except to tell you she spends eight months of the year down in Florida. But you have something very precious with your family, and I was in a position to do something about it."

"So you paid them off? The relationship is only valuable if it's given freely."

Andrew growled in frustration. The physical distance between them allowed her to build walls. Ignoring her protests, he pulled her into his arms. Each twist and turn only served to get her pinned tighter in his embrace.

"Let me go," she demanded.

"Not until I'm finished. You know damned well your father never saw a dime of that money. As for me, I find it a small price to pay so that Tyler could know his family."

She stilled. There was nothing she wouldn't do for her son, so she could hardly argue with his feeling the same way. "You did it for Tyler? No other reason?"

All he had to do was say yes. How easy it would be to agree and end the matter. He couldn't. "Partly."

"And the other part?"

He pushed back the hair that had fallen across her face during her earlier struggle. Although her body was tense, she wasn't fighting him. He considered that progress.

"And you accuse me of being dense. Do you have any idea how much it hurt to see you cry over something that was so easily remedied? I would have paid ten times that amount to see you happy."

"Why?"

"You taught me what it meant to be part of a family, Caitlin. Any gift that special deserves one equally as valuable."

"There's a big difference."

"Monetarily, perhaps. Not in terms of what it meant to me . . . what you mean to me."

"I'm not sure I'm following."

"See if you can follow this. I love you."

"What?"

His arms tightened around her waist and she realized that he was holding her up; her legs had turned to Jell-O again. She was in shock, and Andrew seemed to be amused. The glow from the lights in the distance illuminated his broad smile.

"Am I not speaking clearly, or do you have too much wax in your ears? I said I love you."

Her hearing was fine, but her comprehension was working in slow motion.

"This is where you're supposed to say you love me, too," he said. "Unless, of course, you don't."

The uncertainty in his voice had a sobering effect. He had gone to all that trouble and expense for her, and she had questioned his motives every time. Never once had she given him the benefit of the doubt.

"Don't be absurd."

"Does that mean you love me?"

"Yes."

"Then say it."

She had gone from hell to heaven in the space of three seconds, all because of three little words. Those same three words that people had been trying to pry out of her all day.

"I love you."

"Good. Now we can get a few ground rules straight."

Caitlin let out a choked laugh. No sooner had the words come out of her mouth than Andrew was issuing orders like some mountain man. She should never have let him spend the day with her father.

Where were the passionate kisses and waves of excitement that were supposed to follow declarations of undying love? She was going to cancel his subscription to The Wall. Street Journal and get him a few issues of True Romance. He was going about this love scene all wrong.

"Ground rules?" she repeated.

He shook her shoulders, but with a trace of tenderness. "I don't ever want to hear you refer to yourself as a whore. Is that clear?"

She snuggled closer to him. "Yes, sir."

"As for the money, that is a secret known only to your father and now your brother. Not even Maggie knows. So I don't want to hear it mentioned ever again. You gave me my family. I gave you yours. I'd say that makes us even."

Feeling far too happy to argue, she tipped her fingers

177

to her head in a mock salute. "Yes, sir."

"You owe your father an apology. You said some hurtful things to him. You have no idea how lucky you are to have parents who love you so much, parents who would sacrifice their own happiness to protect you."

Her heart ached at the bitterness laced in his voice. She couldn't change his past for him, but she could make sure that from now on he felt loved.

"And another thing. My employees might call me a bastard, but I didn't like it coming from you. Don't do it again."

She interrupted him playfully. "I'll try, but I'm not making any promises on that one."

He kissed the top of her head. "All right. Next."

"How long is this list?" she moaned wearily.

"I'm not sure. You've always disagreed with everything I've said. While I'm on a roll, I want to keep going."

"Well, hurry it up. I've got other things on my mind besides your needs. Like mine."

She burrowed her hands under his pullover and kneaded the warm flesh of his back. He let out a deep groan. "It seems your needs are irrevocably intertwined with mine."

"I'd say so."

"Is it safe to kiss you?" he asked.

"I might have to take matters into my own hands and physically attack you if you don't."

He kicked his foot along the hard ground. "It could get messy unless you're into twigs and leaves."

"There's an entire field of soft rye grass just beyond that ridge."

"I'm not so out of control that I can't wait until we get back to the hotel."

"You're not? Perhaps this will help." She stroked her fingers over the fly of his jeans, testing his restraint. He groaned and pressed in closer as she cupped her fingers over his erection.

"You deserve better," he muttered against her ear.

178

She shook her head in disagreement. "I already have the best."

* * * *

Sissy's wedding was the social event of Weldon. The rented hall bloomed with floral arrangements on crisp white linen tablecloths. A buffet table at the north end of the room held a wide variety of hot and cold foods all lovingly prepared by friends and family. The sixty guests made it a large gathering by local standards.

Andrew brought two cases of French champagne for the reception. Although Sissy gushed over him for a full ten minutes, Caitlin knew it was a joke directed at her.

"I've been trying to get a dance with you all evening. You've been avoiding me," Andrew said after most of the guests had departed.

Caitlin sighed. "Can you blame me? The last time I drank French champagne and danced with you while one of my sisters got married, I ended up with a baby nine months later."

"I remember. But we sure had fun making him, didn't we?"

Her cheeks flushed hot from the memory. She glanced around the dimly lit room to find her son happily entertained by her mother. She couldn't use Tyler as an excuse. Taking Andrew's hand, she followed him toward the dance floor.

The band was awful, but Andrew didn't notice. All he heard was her soft humming in his ear. She brushed against him and swayed to the music. He was trying to remain dignified in front of her family, but she was sorely testing his restraint

The smooth satin of her ice-blue dress felt as soft as her skin. He had trouble keeping his grip on her shoulder. His hand wanted to slip down along the curve of her back and settle in a place that might shock her parents.

Caitlin, however, made no attempt to behave herself. Her fingers roamed mischievously inside his jacket and down over his buttocks.

He grabbed her wrist "Are you trying to get me in trouble?"

She gazed up at him through her long dark lashes and winked. "Maybe."

"Then you've succeeded." Placing his hands on her shoulder, he turned her around.

John and Sean walked towards them, with hunting rifles in hand. Her giggle turned to outright laughter.

"You think this is funny?" her father asked, hefting his shotgun.

"Sure I do," she said between deep gasps for breath. "Seriously, Andrew, don't you know when you're being put on?"

"This is no joke, young lady," William said gravely.

"Oh, sure. You want me to believe that you plan to put a gun to Andrew's head and demand he marry me."

William stood tall and shot her an indignant glare. "Of course not. I don't want the man to think we're backwoods rubes."

She tilted her head back to look at Andrew. "Told you."

"After all," her father continued. "Andrew is not the problem. You are."

"I beg your pardon?"

"Let me make it clear for you," Andrew said. "They plan to hold the gun to your head until you make an honest man out of me."

She laughed again. "You're as funny as they are."

"Do you see anyone laughing besides yourself?"

"You don't have to marry me."

He wrapped his arms around her waist. "Believe me, Caitlin, I do."

She twisted out of his embrace and whirled around to face him. Her eyes flashed with sparks of anger. "Stop making a joke out of this. It's not funny anymore."

"It's not meant to be funny." He shrugged apologetically and amended, "Well, maybe a little funny, but not a joke."

She blinked and a tear slid down her cheek. "Why not ask like a normal person?"

"Normal doesn't work with you. If I don't do something to get your attention, you don't take me seriously."

"Oh, I take you very seriously. And you've got my attention."

"So will you marry me?"

Her gaze shifted to her father and brother. "Excuse us a moment."

She tugged on Andrew's arm, leading him to a private corner of the room. He followed nervously. Her expression gave nothing away. Was she pleased? Angry? Was she going to decline?

Perhaps he should have waited until they were alone rather than putting her on the spot in front of the family. He might deserve this suspense, but his insides had become a giant knot of tension. "So?" he blurted.

"Yes."

"How soon?" Not the debonair reaction he'd meant to express, but then he'd been confounded by his feelings for her from the very beginning.

She swallowed a nervous cough. "Give me some time to get used to the idea. You never want to wait for anything."

"You take all the time you need, Caitlin." He ran his hand along the small of her back and paused at one of her more sensitive points. His thumb stroked repeatedly over the area until her body trembled. "But while I'm waiting for you to get used to the idea, you'll have to wait for anything beyond a chaste kiss on the cheek."

"Sexual blackmail? That is so unfair," she muttered against his ear.

"Yeah, I know. Especially since I'm so much better at it than you. But, as you once told me, there are no rules in a free-for-all. I'll do whatever it takes to get my way."

Her shimmering eyes reflected a wealth of love. "You're spoiled rotten, Andrew."

"That's your fault."

"My fault? How do you figure that?"

"You're the one who spoiled me. No other woman will do." He lowered his head and took possession of her mouth with every intention of proving it.

The End